TILL WE
MEET
AGAIN

TILL WE MEET AGAIN

SHIBAJI BOSE

Srishti
PUBLISHERS & DISTRIBUTORS

SRISHTI PUBLISHERS & DISTRIBUTORS
Registered Office: N-16, C.R. Park
New Delhi – 110 019
Corporate Office: 212A, Peacock Lane
Shahpur Jat, New Delhi – 110 049
editorial@srishtipublishers.com

First published by
Srishti Publishers & Distributors in 2019

*This book is dedicated to
my father Dipayan Bose,
who will remain the banyan tree
for me, for ever!*

Acknowledgement

When I wanted to quit my job to be on my own, I needed the strength. I needed someone who was convinced and confident to trust me and my commitments. I found it in my wife Aparna. She is my anchor. Whenever I need a purpose to feel accomplished, I find it in my son, Anweshan. When I want someone to smile at me for being whoever I am, I find it in my mother-in-law, Mrs Ila Chatterji. If I need someone to be indifferent to my success and failures, I find it in my mother, Mrs Abha Bose. And when I wish to look for the child I once was, I find it in my brother Swaraj. I acknowledge the presence of the departed souls of my father and my father-in-law in guiding me, if ever, I fumble in the dark.

I acknowledge having received support from my cousin Dr Anirban Bose. My best friends Sushant Dash, Diptanshu Ray and Subrat Behera. Someday, I will write our story. My business partner Malhar for putting up with my tantrums, my closest friend Joydeep Roy for teaching me why and how not to be grumpy. Sarabjit Singh for being my alter ego, Subro Dey for being my fall-back guy, and Amit Kumar Das for instilling in me the value of humility. Some of my all-time positive influencers, which include Mr Sanjoy Sen, Mr Anjan Sengupta, Mr Naval Bir Kumar and Mr Kenneth Andrade. A countless number of my well-wishers, former colleagues, classmates and friends, who have encouraged me to write and are looking forward to read my work. I am fortunate to have found a wonderful guide in my editor, Ms Stuti, and I thank Srishti Publishers for trusting my work and deciding to show it the light of the day.

Prologue

The neighbourhood of Gitanjali in Kolkata woke up every day, accompanied with impatience, and an acknowledging nod from Jeevan to each of his regular patrons. He was found pacifying the fumes from the glasses; rather than justifying the absence of either the flavour or liquor in the re-cycled tea. The tea-stall was orderly and contained in its unwritten membership rules for the regular patrons. The right to admission was reserved on the basis of the exclusivity of topics for discussions; ranging from the retirement rhetoric to diabetic debates, from rheumatic resonance to cardiac congestions.

The regular patrons mentally masturbated on various topics ranging from cricket, politics, inflation and insomnia. So, if and when an occasional intruder or a bystander made any gallant attempt to offer his unsolicited opinion on the topic of discussion for the day, it invited snarl, grunt and disdain from the ghetto of the regular patrons. The topic for the day was women's liberty and emancipation, which according to them was essentially about aping men in their dress, desire and discourses to get acknowledged as an equal.

"Opinions are like arseholes! Each one of us has one, on everything and for everyone." This all conclusive statement from Jeevan was enough to disperse the regulars from his multi-tasking bureau, called the tea-stall. Dismayed at being signalled to be driven away, the patrons would get busy offering finishing touches to the animated discussions that were underway.

Jeevan could well have been into scripting a treatise on multi-tasking, but for the paucity of time. He got ready to dispense the staple breakfast of roti and sabzi for a different set of clientele, who had been conditioned to turn at his stall almost every day without fail. The unquestioned loyalty of this clientele was more on account of the value for money and the harmony of relevance in being a daily wager and lesser for the bland taste that the food was naturally endowed with.

And by the time it was 11.30 a.m., the multi-tasking flair of Jeevan metamorphosed into an office for an adept broker for land, property and houses at the same tea-stall. Rarely did it occur to the regulars at his stall that the finesse with which he used to get them to vacate the place for the next series of transactions was out of contempt and did not have anything to do with extending courtesies. The man had the ingenuity of masking his intent and expression with a deceiving demeanour. It made him remain uncontested in his pursuits as the most sought after in his business despite the presence of his distant compatriots in similar trade.

The neighbourhood of Gitanjali had earned its fame and prominence among its habitants for varied reasons.

Approximately ten years back, the then retired postmaster of the local post office made an unaudited but classified disclosure. Gitanjali featured among the top ten localities in the entire city when it came to the foreign exchange remittance from abroad. It did not come as a surprise to many as most of them were direct beneficiaries.

The warm reception accorded by the off-shore opportunities in the services sector had opened up new and exciting avenues for many young people. Had they chosen to stay back, they would have ended up joining either the ranks and file of political cacophony of despair and despondency, or forced themselves to embrace something remotely relevant to their aptitude.

In the new scenario, the proclamations which were hitherto reserved only for the medical students, the meritorious and the technically inclined careerists, created a level playing field for ordinary mortals. Albeit, at the dismay of the passport office. In other words, it explained the neighbourhood's claim to fame!

The nemesis of simplicity lay in the genesis of inarguably the most prominent profession of middlemanship, more popularly known as '*dalali*'. No other career option had withstood the test of time. But of course with the political patrons not forgetting to extract their share of the booty, arising out of the paperwork and documentation in giving birth to these special classes of citizens called *dalals*.

The neighbourhood remained glued to the possibilities and excitement of a narrative of a chequered simplicity lost in the cosmetic revolution, clamouring to be mentioned as a place for the rich and famous. There were numerous makeshift colonies (*basti*) adjacent to the playgrounds, standing as the solitary guard during the nights. They came alive during the day and through the late evenings as the remarkable identity for each locality that was suitably named either after a deceased statesman or a freedom fighter, e.g. Gandhi colony, Subhash colony, etc.

The earliest signs of the imminent but the definite change became visible when these clubs started getting accessible to the home-grown politicians, who frequented the clubs masquerading as champions of social causes. This ploy was eventually discovered as an easy way to collect subscriptions from the people in finally becoming the local extension of the political parties, baying for the playground to be converted into a gated community of apartments. The mathematics was simple. The clubhouse will become a permanent concrete structure, replete with the gadgets of pleasure, and in the bargain, the club will offer no resistance to the promoters and builders in the erection of multi-storied buildings.

The real estate boom necessitated the presence of a large number of migrant populations who found it convenient to work at the construction site, to eventually become a repository of domestic helps and watchmen for the same project. And then, the middle class would crawl up to their match boxes, politely called apartments. These apartments were considered a witness to the remnant of the last milestone of the middle classes' crumbling pride known as the 'joint family system'.

The alacrity of the conversion of a sleepy neighbourhood to the hustle and bustle of a cosmopolitan city fringe received a boost in the extension of the city's Metro railway's project. Prices started shooting through the roof and you had the banks and the financing companies holding their regular concerts of hawking the competitiveness of housing loans, occasionally offering freebies through lucky draws in the form of mixer grinders, hair dryers and food coupons.

The middlemen started flashing their new business cards as property consultants! This was the time when the farsightedness of some people started taking shape in the form of a change in the dialect of delicacy by starting unconventional food chains. Along with it came the health spas, gymnasiums, upscale western wear franchisees, unisex beauty parlours, pastry shops, digital platforms for grocery and utility delivery at doorstep and the finishing classes in etiquette, grooming and soft skills.

From lingerie and underwear, consumer durables, motor cycle dealers to neon sign-lit rebranded sweet shops, the changes redefined the demography. The change agents started outsmarting the conventional shops smeared with sweat, grime and the frowning crow lines of the ageing shopkeeper to humiliation. Jeevan's tea-stall and the land adjacent were the next to fall in the line. His penchant for a comfortable life gave way to the facelift of the land. The once decrepit tea-stall went on to become a well-equipped food joint.

The law of being an average

A ryan was the eldest of the three siblings. True to the delight of the middle-class tryst with an unqualified testimony in chasing endless dreams, he was born in a family where the pension fund was the recourse to marrying off the daughter. The balance, if any, was meant for building a house. The family was in for a rude shock when they discovered that the legacy of being born, having toiled and getting laid to rest in ignominy, was at threat by the mushrooming of the change agents in the society. Over here, the reason to worry was Aryan's career.

Aryan's father was a medical representative in a pharmaceutical company. By the time Aryan grew up to become a young adult, and much to his delight, he found his father paying infrequent visit to their home once a month. The nature of his job required him to be on official tours. Announcing the discomfort of an average academic score to his father was such a certainty, that it was no longer considered as an act of bravado by his classmates. Aryan's father was very sure of him in becoming just another face in the crowd, while

Aryan insisted upon himself that he was sure of something extraordinary to happen with him.

During Aryan's graduation, his father got relocated back to the city and made his presence felt at home. Aryan realised the law of being an average required him to defend himself with an attitude of dissidence to his father's insistence that he was actually a moron. What surprised Aryan during the once a week ritual of his father's disdainful observations about him, was his mother's stupor and the silence. He kept wondering if his mother was subscribing to the fact of his being worthless or was she waiting with bated breath in measuring the miracles of tomorrow, when his father would be proved incorrect in his estimation of Aryan.

Aryan did not consider his mother either to be a timid lady or as someone docile to the restlessness of his father's pronouncements. He, however, considered his mother's subservience to be an act of circumventing her own set of protests in having single-handedly raised a family of three children in an arrangement of convenience with his father consummated in the social act of marriage.

When she left the battleground for Aryan to be slaughtered with the verbal abuse, she did make him feel that resilience was indeed a virtue and a powerful act of defiance to be engaged with, at that point in time. The woman was fighting all her battles, knowing that the war was not yet over!

In these frequent ensembles of emotions that got staged every now and then, Aryan had noticed that his younger brother Rohan was growing up to be a sensible man in having already internalized the law of *how to not become an average,* well ahead of his time. And thus, he seldom was at the receiving end; be it praise or the pain. Rohan was younger to him in age, but much wiser. The youngest of the three siblings, Rhea was a tender version of their mother in her conduct, reception and opinions as well.

"Come aside and I will explain why you come across as worthless," Rohan thrust their father's business card at Aryan's face. "What do you see and what do you read?" Aryan drew a blank as explained. "Our father is still a medical representative that he was twenty-five years back and that explains his dejection and dismay with himself. He vents his failure as a father and as a careerist in not having been successful in either of the roles. You being the eldest, he personifies his lost pride in your remaining an average and thus you are almost always at the receiving end."

Rohan's wisdom and interpretation kept resonating with Aryan throughout the day, as he began to build the blocks of his perceptions about his father, whose sense of accomplishment was etched in Aryan's success. His father's self-actualization forced him to accept that he was a failure as a father and as a careerist. That had made him to become unreasonably stubborn with himself and with everyone around.

This sense of self-deprecation when got added to the fact that Aryan was average in his academics, made his father fight his inner demons. But in the process, he became the demon for Aryan! But wasn't it late for Aryan to re-discover the certainty that was in store for him? Or, was it the same vibe of resilience that he had been receiving from his mother all along in measuring the miracle of a tomorrow? She was braving the battles with the hope that she would eventually emerge victorious in the war.

At twenty-three years of age, and without a job after his graduation, a specific event reassured Aryan to relook at him with some measured risks. He accompanied Rohan to a career fair and found himself rediscovering the purpose of becoming someone. The world had not changed a bit. What had changed was the way of looking at it.

The fairground was teeming with young people in their flights of fancy, while making attempts to understand their career options. The traditional options were attracting the meritorious while the unconventional ones were inviting the experimentally brave, the critical pessimists or the creative mediocre. One such career stall caught his attention and Aryan found himself registering for the career counselling session in grooming and styling.

Back at home, Aryan found himself at loss of words to join the conversation with the family which required him to explain his pursuits at the career fair. Rohan stole the show with his excitement at having collected the brochures of various business schools as against the banter and the jab at Aryan's choice for the grooming and styling career. Aryan missed out on his mother mutter something, which by itself was an act of rarity at the dinner table, considering the situation when he was in front of the entire family.

"Speak out, let your father know about your interest area and what do you wish to be?"

Aryan reciprocated spontaneously to the invite and announced, "I want to be a stylist, a hair stylist."

Rhea was helping her mother to collect the soiled plates from the table, and spoke for everyone else, "Not a bad idea as a starter!"

That was followed with their father offering slightest resistance, which surprisingly was the first as an instance itself. But he took digs at him, laced with sarcasm. "Rohan, you could have avoided asking Aryan to accompany you to the career fair. Considering the fact that even a recommendation from me would not be enough for him to land a job in my pharmaceutical firm, I am glad that you explored options for your own career."

"Your father has decided to hand over our property to Raghav, who is a well-known promoter and developer in Gitanjali, to build a multistoried complex. Aryan, start looking out for a temporary place on rent for us to move out till the project gets completed, for us to move back, to one of the apartments in the complex," his mother intervened to divert the discussion.

The father drew a close to the conversation for the day. "The days are changing, and having considered the price that this land will fetch, I thought it is wise to sell off the land and retain an apartment spacious enough for all of us, in addition to a decent amount of money to marry off Rhea and pay for Rohan's management studies."

Aryan did not even feature in the monstrous relief of embracing the inevitability of owning a part of the fortune. He was expected to disown the stigma of being an average that was attached to him and his abilities to be even considered for a discussion. However, it did occur to him that the certainty of a secured tomorrow for the family did work wonders in having instilled a sense of sanity in the choice of words that got exchanged at the dinner table. Most importantly, he spoke for himself, however trivial it may have been to others. He did speak for himself!

Aryan's impatience for the day to break was hardly noticed by anyone but by his mother. "Do not forget to hunt for the place on rent when you are out. Let your father know of the fee to be paid for whatever styling and grooming class that you have decided to pursue." She was crisp and to the point, as brevity was the virtue in her perseverance to wait for the tomorrow to win the war.

The day indeed was different as Aryan chose to notice the neighbourhood, which had changed so much in the last one decade of his growing up as a kid. He remembered getting avoided by his playmates because he was nowhere close to be counted as academically meritorious.

Aryan arrived at the styling school, magnificent by its imposing glass facade sprung up in the place of an erstwhile tea-stall that once belonged to Jeevan. It included the adjoining land which was once the playground for the club; the same club that celebrates the Durga puja festivities once a year, blessed with the grandeur of the real estate money from the local land shark Raghav; who one hears is bracing up for his second innings as a politician.

The best part of being an average is that you're rarely overwhelmed and that's exactly what happened to Aryan upon entering the reception. It was resplendent with the richness of a designer appeal to act as a decoy in fleecing the uninitiated, at the speed and pace with which the morality was losing its grounds to the impropriety of values. Aryan was ushered into a cosy corner to a designated counsellor as he kept on shifting helpless glances amidst the unfamiliar terrain of sophistication.

"Hi, good morning. I am Priya, your counsellor for the course. Thank you for coming."

What followed during the next few minutes was a symphony of inebriated day dreaming by an adult, whose mirror was untrue to him in reminding of the man in him. Priya was impressionably pretty. She was striking a fine balance between the traditional curvatures of a deity, infused with the confidence of a modern woman in her early thirties.

Aryan woke up to the deceit of a compliment for having decided upon one of the more rewarding career options. Priya assured him that even a day's delay to get him enrolled for the course would have meant nothing less than forfeiting the career opportunity of a lifetime. Aryan felt blessed and for reasons known to him, thanked Rohan for having escorted him to the career fair.

He regained his composure with the blaring and honking of the horns in the peak business hours during the day that separated the imposing building which would be his classroom for the next six months. He, however, had to justify the fifty thousand rupees fees to his father. It was an entry to the surreal world of Priya and her tribe to escape from the drudgery of a self-imposed perception and the persecutions that followed.

In the meanwhile, the uprising that was unfurling across the state was shooting up as a sharp and uninterrupted gradient in the political milieu with every passing day. The graph became a plateau on the day when the electorate decisively voted for the change in the state's political leadership and it was to be left onto the leadership of the new government to give an upward direction to the graph. The electorate chose to uproot a three-decade old economically irrelevant and ideologically defunct political class in favour of a promised change. Celebration for change had its own ramifications in the form of stubbornness.

On that fateful day when the mascot of decadence was making its last attempt to hold onto their revered fort, a violent clash ensued between the victorious and the vanquished. In the cross fire that followed between the police and the pompous pageant of people's mandate, many were left injured and one dead.

The smoke was blowing into bellowing rings in the air and this time it was from the incense sticks. The pace at which the events were unfolding in the last few days were nothing less than a soulful drama for the family who were till the other day rejoicing the impending joy of a certainty in their lives. They were now given in to mourning the loss of a life.

The corpse that came back home was that of Aryan's father.

It was Aryan's first visit to the crematorium. He was immediately caught up with witnessing of the unique grieving and the monstrous wailing faces along with the covetousness of the uncertainty as the fallout of a loss! The embers from the electric crematorium, unmindful of the stench of the burnt human flesh kept belching out the black fumes with the dexterity that can be identified only with a machine. The facade of the personal loss manifested into the 'rites of living'.

The pronouncement of death triggered a series of rituals associated with it. Firstly, it was the doctor at their house. He was adjusting his stethoscope, not because of the bewilderment in calming the nerves of the family, but silently endorsing the maintaining of a stony endeavour but not forgetting to claim the 'fee' for signing the death certificate. The next was the assortment of every possible tell-tale sign in the use and abuse of floral fragrance and the rickety bed which is accepted more for its resale value and less for its aesthetics. It was followed by the arrival of the hearse bedecked with the name of the sponsors and their emblems.

The spontaneity with which a corpse is ushered into the crematorium makes the grief take a second seat to the dash in queuing up for the *first come, first served* rule at the 'rights of admission reserved' platform for cremation. This is the place where the right to live ends up to become the rites of living.

The dead body coming from grandeur of mansions, maids and Mercedes finds a place beside the tarpaulin inhabiting footpath dweller. It draws the similarity in death being the final destination where discrimination finds no place but for the lexicon of mortals.

The priest keeps a watchful eye as a scavenger would on the residue of what used to be 'living' and now being 'dead'. But, not forgetting the accompanying grief mongers along with the corpse in extracting the right price for creating a passage to the next world. Under pricing is forbidden, over pricing is cursory and the right price for rituals never gets established.

The next to fall in line are the extortionists by birth and profession. A sect of people with blood-shot eyes, who have accepted to being termed as the 'scavengers' for customary rituals associated with the funerals and ash-digging. They have perfected the art of turning flesh to ashes with or without the electric crematoriums. The price for performance is discussed between the family and the accompanying grievers to finalize the transaction to be formalised either in a penny or by the pound.

The forty-five minutes of the flesh-to-ash act get witnessed by everyone who has by then grouped themselves into small huddles that clearly separated the friends and colleagues from the relatives. Each of these huddle has a defined agenda for discussion over the steaming cups of tea.

Aryan was being extended commiseration from a friend of his father, while the others got into mourning the genuine loss of a life. Some of them were discussing the after-effects of death on the life and times of the dependents, as some went on discussing the equitable distribution of the legacy in wealth and property. Some of the relatives accompanying Aryan to the crematorium were debating on the legality of the surrogate, if any, to the share of the deceased.

In the meanwhile, some well-wisher would have already dialled and booked the venue to commemorate the death. And, there were a handful among the mourners who were in two minds, as to whom do they approach for the return fare from the crematorium to their residence.

Amazing, perplexing and the real discoveries in appointing the 'death' as the precursor to 'life' as usual for all of those who survived the scare and the inevitability of death. The stamp, seal and sign by the registrar at the crematorium became the empirical evidence of the demise.

Lives would continue as usual, along with the greed, dishonour and decay for all the tall claims that would be made in the obituary, if at all. The rituals and rites meant for the dead would no longer matter to anyone in their pursuit of living; but for the wall, on which the framed picture would alter the décor, a bit!

The father was conspicuous with his absence in abuse but Aryan rued his loss and went into a path of self-discovery in having been anointed with the responsibilities that evaded him when his father was alive. He chanced upon the briefcase in which his father used to carry his merchandise for the appointment with the doctors. It had the cheques books, life insurance details neatly compiled into a note along with the mention of files and documents of his retirement, contacts and an envelope that had Aryan's name written on it. Aryan took out the envelope carefully and noticed that it was written recently, closer to the date when his father left them all to be on their own.

Dear Aryan,

Having watched you grow is the single biggest sense of accomplishment for fatherhood. The experiences may vary from one father to another, but each of us as a father takes an inexplicable pride in having reared a thoroughbred bloodline. Your birth was a personification of feelings that ranged from a sense of enhanced responsibility, pride, inter-dependence and love, as you completed the cycle of my life.

I am sure that my father would have experienced similar emotions when I came into his life. I must have outgrown him by the size of the shoes that I wear today and yet, many a times I yearn to cuddle up to the warmth of his unrequited love and the silent reciprocation. But, he is no more!

I do not know what stopped me when I was of your age from telling my father how much I admired him. I do not know what came in between me and my father when it was about letting everyone know that we completed the circle of each other's lives. Was it the fear of a rebuttal that just did not exist? Was it

*the typical growth pang that paralyzed the admission
by an adult for his father? Or, was just that I did not
make an attempt?*

*A sense of guilt lurks somewhere in me which
compels the selfishness in me to assuage my ability
to admit that I loved my father. I want you to know
that I will keep longing for your selfless love. I want
you to be a father to me now. I want you to foster
within me, the sense of responsibility, pride, inter-
dependence and admiration. These are the things that
I have lost out in the forlorn pursuit of relationships
that will never ever substitute my personal loss. I feel
abandoned in the realm of a stupor, when I try to seek
but fail to reach out to him.*

*I may have come across as tyrannical and
overbearing for I let the fool in me, at times, to intrude
into your space when you had already become an
adult. You must have understood it to be the dark
side in me. I was actually trying to be the father,
fortifying his words and the acts of self-acclaimed
wisdom, which I agree should have been avoided.
I must have come across at times, a self-appointed
apostle of virtues, righteousness and conduct which
must have made you to smirk at the mirror, but for
me, it was simply an act of wanting to see all those
things in you which are missing in me.*

*I will grow older and I will talk more. I will put
on dentures and will be short of hearing. I will get*

myopic and possibly get intolerant of your ways and means. I will try to defend the traditions that will make you shy away and consider disowning me. I will wait for you to join me at the dinner table, when you might be already in the company of your beloved.

But I will keep in mind that these could be the reasons that you do not yearn to cuddle up to the warmth of my unrequited love and the silent admission of the fact that you have grown up to become a man. Be my son, however old you grow, and let me remain a father to you as we complete the circle for each other's life.

Here's with all my love for you Aryan,

Baba

By the time Aryan was through with reading the letter, he found Rhea beside him, touching his shoulders lightly in admission of the loss of their father, who may have been purely misunderstood all these years. Aryan was sobbing when Rhea took him into her arms and then the overwhelming emotions completely overtook his brooding silence as he started crying out inconsolably. Solitude was what he was looking and Rhea ensured that no one went to him in offering company to his melancholy. The family had found the new *man in their house.*

Aryan was asked to wait outside Raghav's office. He noticed that the weekly assembly outside his office consisted of people coming to the builder-turned-politician with prayers. Ranging from addressing land and property disputes, the pleas also consisted of seeking employment opportunities, protection from the police harassesment and in getting applications actioned upon for civic repairs. Aryan's agenda was entirely different from the beeline of hapless devotees at Raghav's temple.

By the time Aryan got to see the man, it was already late in the day and Raghav was getting ready to come out of his *durbar*. He, however, chose to notice Aryan and paused to hear one of his aides narrate the recent woes that had befallen the family after the death of their father.

Raghav had done well in life to become a city slicker in expressing his sympathy, but with a frown in his forehead. "So, have you come up looking for a job or are you looking for a letter to expedite the retiral claims from your father's office?"

"I have come here to complete the process of moving to a rented place and to collect the documents that you had got my father to sign, in developing and promoting the land."

Raghav was unnerved as he caught his personal aide unprepared. "Did you not tell this young man that I do not conduct business at this hour and in this place?" Turning to Aryan, he barked at him. "You come and see me in my office in the evening."

And with an air of indifference, he waved at the people and rode off in his car. Something was clearly amiss with the diffidence Aryan faced in the brief encounter with Raghav. But he felt good at not having run for a cover during the face off!

On returning home, Aryan found Rohan obstinately shouting at Rhea, looking threatening with his finger raised at her. Aryan took no time in questioning Rohan. His voice sounded authoritative, with the coldness of ice and assertive with responsibility. Rohan held onto his fort for sometime, but yielded at the face of the new-found man of the house in Aryan. Rhea narrated the entire account which had led to the squabble between her and Rohan.

Soon after, the family was through with the rites and the rituals of mourning. Rohan had sought an audience with Raghav to further his studies. In lieu of ten lakh rupees, he had got a set of documents signed by their mother. It absolved the seasoned crook in Raghav to pay for the rental for a makeshift accommodation till such time that the property got developed in their land. They were actually entitled to an apartment as was originally agreed between their deceased father and Raghav.

Aryan held on to his composure during the narrative of a deceit and so did their mother. She came up all of a sudden to slap hard at Rohan's face and then plonked on the chair. Rhea left the room to others, fretting and fuming at the orderly chaos that was making the family vulnerable in drifting apart from one another. Rhea had nursed her own set of dreams to be married off and start a family of her very own.

A frugal dinner forced itself as a lump at Aryan's throat, when his mind was attempting at solving the myriad puzzles. He could not force himself taking an offence with Rohan's decision, but at the same time, he did not ignore the crow lines across his mother's face. What was killing him was Rhea's silence, as if she had become the proverbial sacrificial goat at the altar of the recent developments. The fallout of Rohan's admission was heavy enough to outwit the options that they were left with to carry on with their lives. It was time for Aryan to act.

The next morning, Aryan reached Raghav's office that was well suited to conduct business in leveraging his political affiliations. The office had greater number of suitors in remarkable attires with their files and documents waiting for a stamp of approval for various government tenders and contracts.

He was a little surprised when he was asked to meet Raghav well ahead of others and was in for a greater shock when he was received with an acknowledging smile. Raghav thrust a big brown envelope and smiled wryly. "This concludes our business." Aryan took out the documents and carefully studied the contents which had the agreement and a power of attorney signed by his mother amending the original agreement in favour of Raghav's claim.

It occurred to Aryan that the slap on Rohan's face on the previous evening was actually an acknowledgement by his mother to have been meticulously duped in signing the document. It was a carefully drafted agreement to vacate their place of residence in a month's time. Aryan returned back the smile in all the earnestness of concluding the business for then, but not before serving a parting remark, "I will laugh the loudest, for I will laugh at last."

A lot was required to be done and at a frenzied pace of outsmarting the unnerving events that took place in the last one month. It was not difficult to find the place on rent, which was the ground floor of a two-storied house that became their address. The next ordeal was to gather the confidence in meeting the officials at his father's office to work out the settlement. It fortunately was more of a pleasant experience; thanks to the people he had met at the crematorium.

Aryan had one more important task to attend to before he could carry on with rediscovering himself with the newer pursuits to confront life. He had to meet Priya at the styling and grooming school to formally communicate his inability in pursuing the course and seek a refund of the course fee.

Moving to the new place was an uneventful one; although it took them some time to accept the sobriety of the fact that they would now have some additional people meddling with their lives. Rhea had resumed her classes to appear for her higher secondary examinations while Rohan had already decided on the institute to pursue his studies. Their mother went about carrying on as usual, without any complaints, but occasionally seeking solace in the company of other women who flocked the local temple in the evenings. The women discussed their lives and events and it sounded very similar to her battles.

The day arrived when Rohan was ready to leave for his studies. His excitement was bereft of any remorse. Undaunted with the pride of a pleasant tomorrow, he was dissociating himself with all the events and the people that were a part of his yesterday. He was bracing for a tomorrow in eluding the family bonds of today.

Aryan's checklist

It was for the first time Aryan found himself spending so much time in the front of the mirror. He had his own share of fantasies while growing up, but being a recluse by nature, his fantasies were frequented only by the women either from the immediate neighbourhood or the girls from his college. His dreams had him playing truant to one cinematic illusion after another as his filmy heroines frolicked in their skirts, prancing around the trees with Aryan. But they always made it a point to ride away on a bike with some other heroes!

On his way out, his mother handed him the wallet which was originally carried by his father. One of his few prized possessions along with some more documents. He had to complete the formalities of declaring the death of his father and get himself to sign as the joint account holder along with his mother for all the banking related transactions.

He completed the formalities at the bank, which confirmed a balance of twenty lakh rupees after the encashment of six lakhs by Rohan towards his admission with Ranchi

Management School. Aryan walked out of the bank and noticed the imposing SUV of Raghav in front of the cafeteria opposite the bank. It whizzed past him and so did the pretty face of a maiden beside Raghav, unmindfully scourging the scorching sun.

Aryan reached the imposing building and walked up the flight of stairs to reach the reception. And there was Priya in her unscathed appeal, talking to a prospective student. Aryan approached the reception and asked for an appointment with Priya. He chose to wait for Priya over the ready availability of another counsellor, plunging into another romance in broad daylight. It must have been an hour of waiting when he was led to Priya's work station.

She looked up at him and gestured him to take the seat opposite her. He was getting fidgety with the documents, noticing which, Priya comforted him with a welcome chide. "So Aryan, what made you to think that you can skip your classes?" Aryan's encounter with the rebuke was a spontaneous apology along with the explanation for his absence. Priya heard him out and without the slightest of hesitation conveyed to him that he may opt to attend the classes immediately or forfeit the fees in entirety.

It could have been either the candidness of the conversation or the conviction of having checked the bank account that made Aryan mumble out to sound like a lamb in the den of the tigress. "I will come to the classes from tomorrow."

Priya noticed the discomfiture in Aryan and chose to sound reassuring. "It is a matter of six months and once you complete your course, I will assist you in getting to work with a salon."

The affirmation in her voice and the assurance of a certainty in finding a job was a soothing balm to his nervousness as he committed his first sin of taking the offer at the face value. It was after all the being made by Priya! Aryan had his classes three days in a week, for three hours. Not that it mattered much for someone as unoccupied as him, but he longed for those three days, as it gave him the opportunity to steal a glance or two at Priya.

From the cuts, curls, sleek and straight to the up dos, layers, volumes and waves, Aryan got himself to learn the craft of slithering his fingers across the weird wigs in perfecting the art of styling and grooming. The craft required him to wield the accessories with the alert and the deftness of a surgeon at work. The sprays, thermal mousse, gels, heat tamers and the brushes were the reasons to celebrate his self-discovery at the end of each class. He was, in fact, enjoying the admiration of his classmates and the masters with each passing day. He was immersed in learning the art as an apprentice waiting for the centre stage in the days to come.

Aryan completed his certificate course which coincided with Rhea's higher secondary results, and they had reasons to celebrate the small success story to overcome the grimness which had otherwise cast its gloomy spell in their lives. The brother-sister duo decided to shop for dinner. The simplicity of this happiness made them eschew the fact that the last time they celebrated as a family was during Rohan's birthday.

They were through with their shopping for the utilities and came to the bus stop to take an autorickshaw back home when Aryan noticed Priya at the stop. It was late in the afternoon and the humidity in the air was making it uncomfortable. She was wiping off the shiny gleaming beads of perspiration from her forehead. Aryan was playing a protective brother in balancing the bags and holding on to Rhea's hand. Rhea was so infatuated with her recent success that she was invariably stomping either on something or someone while walking.

It took some time for Aryan to decide if he would get them introduced to each other as Priya was looking considerably disturbed, visibly ill at ease, waiting in the sun. He let go off the triviality of an introduction, but could not help notice the admiration in Rhea's eyes for the pretty face that was clearly an exception at the bus stop. And then the SUV stopped, just short of running over them, while Priya hopped onto it.

Aryan's face grimaced with despair and pain in recollecting the pretty face in the same SUV a few days ago, whizzing past the bank, scourging at the scorching sun. Rhea, who was admiring the pretty face a few minutes back, held onto her breath in helping Aryan get back to his feet to collect the bags that got dropped in the unpreparedness of the event. It was the same dream, but this time, his heroine had chosen to ride off in an SUV instead of a bike!

On their reaching home, they found their mother neatly attired in a cotton sari, holding forth sweets for both of them. She had pride written all over her face for Rhea and perhaps for Aryan as well, but her eyes were searching for Rohan.

Aryan received his first gift from his mother in a long time, a cell phone, while Rhea went ecstatic finding her new wares, clothes and accessories, including a brand new back pack and basic cosmetics.

In the collective smiles that followed, Rhea remarked, "Imagine a stylist at home; grooming his sister for the college everyday. Ma, your days are over and now bhaiya will be styling me instead of your plain and monotonous plaits of hair with black, green and red ribbons. I am a college going girl now."

Sensing the plight of untold miseries of a mother, Aryan enquired about Rohan, if he might have made any call. "Rohan has a phone and I have his number which he had shared in his last letter, written well over two months ago. Now that you have a cell phone, why don't you call him to find it out for yourself?" Self effacing and elusive to exhibit any kind of fragility in her emotions, Aryan knew his mother well, but when it came to her children, she always chose to own up her susceptibility of being a mother.

"Hello Rohan. How have you been? You know what, I have completed my styling and grooming course and waiting for a job. Rhea has cleared her exams with flying colours and will be attending her college very soon. Ma has gifted me a cell phone. You must store this number and call me at your convenience."

"Aryan, I am pursuing my business management and I do not expect you to understand the rigours. Pass on my regards to Ma and my congratulations to Rhea. It is not possible for me to call you every now and then as I am very busy with my studies. Ask mother to send me another six thousand for this month."

"But Ma has already paid such a huge sum for your admissions, and then she has been paying your monthly expenses?"

"What about my toothpaste and biscuits? What about my books and stationeries? Aryan, it's time you get into a job and start earning for the family. You have been sitting at home, minding no business at all."

"Ok, Rohan I will talk to Ma and work out something. You take care of yourself."

Aryan took no offence to what transpired between him and Rohan as a conversation, as he did not want to run away from the harsh facts. Yes, he had been without work for almost two years now, after his graduation. Rhea's education, marriage and reclaiming the apartment from Raghav, which rightfully belonged to them, in addition to working out a regular monthly income for the family, were Aryan's immediate priority and the checklist!

Aryan was accompanying Rhea to her college. She had applied to study mass communication at the college of her choice. With her score, it was not much difficult to seek admission to the college. While walking past the place that was once a house to them, he noticed that the entire house had been pulled down and got replaced with concrete pillars in announcing the arrival of yet another gated community in Gitanjali. It reminded him of the task that lay ahead of him to wrest back the documents and the ownership of an apartment.

They hurried past the banner announcing the twenty-four hours security with a close circuit camera, lift, firefighting and the play area for children, along with a community hall that would be coming up at the place. Aryan was consciously ticking an invisible checklist of tasks that the new-found responsibility had earmarked for him.

He had worked out the monthly expenses along with his mother, after having accounted for the rental and the regular monthly expenses. His basic sense of calculation rang an alarm bell that the bank balance could take care of the entire family for the next three years, after earmarking a decent sum towards Rhea's marriage. Time was fast outpacing the little spurts of happiness with a sense of urgency that left him wondering if he had the luxury of trials and errors to look out for a career. He realized that he needed a job as of yesterday!

The next morning, Aryan forced himself out of the bed. It was unusually early for him. The early morning had a promise of plenty which made him wonder the loss of many such days when he had very little to offer to the day. He remembered the days gone by when the sounds of the household chores would break the quietness of the previous night. While his sibling got ready for her share of the day, he kept lying in bed as he kept himself occupied with and irritably repetitive dreams knowing well that *she* would eventually ride off on the bike.

He got off to a start with a sense of urgency that he learnt and picked up while talking to Rohan the previous night, which he had kept to himself. He was in the streets in no time. Aryan's primary sense of self-reasoning made him walk towards his styling school to accost Priya on her promise of an engagement after completing the course.

He was armed with a reason while ignoring the imposing glass facade of the building that housed his classes, to walk up to the reception enquiring about Priya's whereabouts. A mechanical voice informed him over the reception that she had left her job a few days back for better prospects elsewhere.

Aryan would have marched off unannounced but for his new-found sense of urgency which surprised him as he demanded to meet any other counsellor available. A matronly lady met him, who was nowhere close to Priya's debauchery that she had hid in her garb of plain speaking. The woman came across as righteously curt. She explained to him the difference between placement guarantee and assistance as Aryan started scribbling his personal details in the placement assistance form.

Interestingly, he was not cursing anyone, not even his fate as he was fiercely determined to land himself with a job. The lady finding an uncharacteristic lack of resistance from Aryan offered him with a parting assurance. "We will get in touch with you, the moment any employer shows interest in your profile." The barrenness of her assurance was directed at placating his discomfort in not finding a promise being fulfilled.

He took very little cognisance of her assurance and instead asked, "Where do I find Priya?" He had put the question as he was sure of not accommodating any further ambiguity in his search for a job. The lady volunteered the information upon catching the fervent appeal in his eyes, which were no longer helpless but confident with what he wanted with himself.

"Priya is now a big shot at the RGV Enterprises. Try your luck for an appointment."

The turn of events during the day was gradually fortifying his relentless self-conviction to resurrect himself out of a void. He strode off the office without replying or acknowledging the information from the lady, but not before catching her smirk at the state of his affairs. On the streets, but with a sense of purpose, he found his inner self making peace with himself. He knew that he was cornered, but he had very little to lose as he was raring to break the mould of having been an average.

Aryan scouted for a place in the wilderness of the unknown faces where he wanted some time for himself as he chanced upon Jeevan's food joint. It was recently refurbished with the real estate boon announcing the dexterity of transactions from the men and machines alike; vending snacks and beverages to the voracious appetite of the people for junk food. The once rickety thatched bamboo stall now served fast food options, employing assistants and cooks while Jeevan was busy with the cash register ringing every minute. What a man!

Aryan searched for Jeevan's regular clients, but found none as they were long gone. Quite possibly confined either to their graves or have passed the baton of patronage to a considerably younger group of people in their late twenties or early thirties. Those are the ones who were frequenting the food joint, flaunting their conquest of gadgets, gears and girls.

Having realised that looking for an empty corner was going to be a luxury, Aryan settled for sipping a cup of tea, trying to figure out the animated discussions in a group. One of them definitely was the boss as others were nodding in approval to his wild gestures. They were discussing credit cards, leads, prospects and targets. The team was relatively young, consisting of men and women barely out of their colleges, eager to take a head-start with their lives.

The pensive look had graduated to an uncomfortable stare and by the time he could correct himself, he found the boss waving at him. Aryan came up to the man. "Do we know each other or would you want me to know you?"

Aryan nodded sheepishly at the piercing eyes of the man in question who was a few years above his age as he muttered back, "I am looking for a job, do you have one to offer?"

"I am Arvind and we have jobs for anyone who can break into a conversation with strangers. If you are genuinely looking at breaking the ice, come to this place in the evening at 8.00 p.m. and I will see how good you are with your words and overcoming your inhibitions."

Aryan was overcome with some relief till he passed by 'Aesthetics', the luxurious unisex salon and spa, when it occurred to him that his sense of personal accomplishment and gratification was destined at becoming a stylist. But for then, he consciously ticked off another item in the checklist of his immediate priorities at hand. He had little clue how to prepare and present himself to Arvind in the evening. The only question that kept popping up and bothered him was how to appear for his first interview amidst the crowd.

By the time he was back home, he found Rhea busy with their mother, narrating her eventful day at college. The most remarkable development for the day was however reserved for their mother's pronouncement, that she had been to the bank along with their landlord and that henceforth she was to be considered comfortable with conducting regular banking by both of them. Another battle won by the woman!

Aryan decided it wise not to disclose what happened with him during the day, till he had a confirmation of the job in hand. He spent the next few hours arranging his papers and even went on to neatly compose a hand-written job application. It was 7.30 p.m. as Aryan walked out of the house to demystify the tryst in store for him.

Fighting battles to win the war

The neighbourhood looked spanking in the bright lights. The notoriety of the automobiles in the ever-diminishing roads kept on reminding him of the speed at which the entire world was moving around him. Something that he had been missing out, till Rohan woke him up from his deep slumber of having resigned himself to be counted as an average.

The men and women were hurrying back home as the parade of a leisurely crowd hopping from groceries shops to the stationery stores. From the absentminded stare of the ATM kiosk's guard at the customer withdrawing thick wads of currency notes to the carefree pillion riders on the bikes with their low waist denims fashionably showing off their undergarment brands.

The entire world was moving around him in an undeclared frenzy of rejoicing the renouncement of a riddle called life! The entire world was spontaneously celebrating each and every fringe reason considered to be an event. The idea was to decisively run away from any invisible trace of despondency associated with the realities known and understood as *living a life.*

Aryan chose to wait while scanning the surroundings. It was well past 8.00 p.m. and there was no sign of Arvind. Although he wasn't exactly impatient, Aryan was pacing the place to get over with the ordeal. He wanted a job confirmation in his hand. The shimmering SUV made a grand entry and a couple of people jumped out of it from the front as Aryan did not miss out in catching a glimpse of Priya, who was seated alongside Raghav at the back.

The stooges ran back to the vehicle carrying the finger food and the tea. Priya looked dignified while sipping the beverage. She was in her new role as a big shot with the RGV Enterprises. She casually stole a glance at Aryan while handing over the cup to the flunkies. A pat at his back and Aryan turned around to find Arvind, while Priya rode off the SUV. What followed next was a measured conversation in which Arvind started briefing Aryan on the modalities of selling credit cards. By the time Aryan regained his composure, he was asked to start working from the very next day.

He did not fumble with his words to put up his set of questions at Arvind. "Would you like to check my papers and certificates?"

"In our line of conducting business, the street smart, self-confident do not cling on to their academic averages. They go about invading the privacy of people known as the prospects in making a statement to close the sale."

Aryan silently reasoned the taut and aggressive remark by Arvind and settled with a conviction. This is it! Nobody cares to listen, go ahead and make a noise to be heard!

"And, when do I collect my appointment letter? And the salary?"

Hearing this, Arvind twisted his face and came up with an impoverished sneer, taking a dig at his self-esteem with so much of contempt that it made Aryan reconsider at wallowing in self pity.

"Salary, my dear friend will be earned when you pick up ten documents during a month; out of which there must be a minimum of four conversions. You get to earn 8,000/- for a month and anything less renders you ineligible for the dole. I accommodate non-performance for three months and then you may watch the best of motivation videos on YouTube to become the next Apple, Gates or Ambani all by yourself. This is the only profession that does not come with an entry barrier."

Arvind came across as a ruthless lunatic and self obsessed with his own set of righteousness, but Aryan found his words articulating very simple and basic aspects of life. Arvind's wisdom of handling the adversities of life was all about grounded checks and binds in preparing the uninitiated to accept the terms with humility.

"I will work for you," Aryan baulked.

"You do not work for me; you get to work with me and from right now," Arvind barked.

Arvind handed him some product brochures and asked him to approach the strangers randomly to seek time from them in completing the formalities of selling the credit card. Aryan was throbbing with an excitement of unknown as he gathered the brochures and went about meeting one person after another, handing out the brochures.

He must have met a dozen of them when he found that the brochures were finding a place either at the trash or being left behind, crumpled along with the leftover at the tables. He came back to Arvind who was engrossed with his team of young men and women, discussing their individual conquests of the day.

"Why do you think you are back without a single appointment? It is because, all of those people saw through the self-pity in your appeal, begging and pleading for time. You failed because none of them found any value in your proposition as they were occupied with prevailing over your pitiful state of being, while shooing you off. You are definitely not the guy I am looking to work with."

Aryan's self-discovery came at the cost of plundering a faint hope of landing a job, but he was thankful that the lessons on life had begun; albeit late, but for sure. His mind kept wondering. Now, what was in it for me? Back at home he forced himself a smile at Rhea's continuous chatter of how she was getting popular by each day with her classmates and the faculty and how she was getting chosen for various interesting assignments and field work. Aryan's single biggest achievement till date was living a life in self-denial as he started drawing inspiration from Rhea's excitement.

Self-castigated as a mediocre, Aryan tried to remember any incidence of growing up with the brazenness and irresponsibility of a normal youth. It must be the self-pity which made the world to avoid him for good. Aryan wanted to grow, grow up fast and earnestly prayed to all the deities thronging the wooden replica of a temple that adorned his mother's room, which she shared with Rhea.

He was talking to the deities, "I do not have a friend; I do not have a foe either. I do not remember competing with anyone at school and college, no one ever considered me a worthwhile contender for any crown, be it at academics or any other pursuits for that matter. I forced myself to believe that remaining aloof will help me grow up unnoticed of my inadequacies and today I am clamouring for limelight. It is so suffocating living the life of a hermit. I want to break free!"

Aryan looked at the breaking of dawn. His dreams were so difficult during the previous night, but it was so different that it seemed as if he had broken the cocoon to metamorphose into what he wanted out of himself in life. Coming out of the house, he came across their landlord minding his kitchen garden. It was almost a year that they had moved to this place and he doubted if he had ever exchanged any pleasantry with the gentleman or his family. It was no longer an instance of self-pity when he walked up to greet the landlord.

The gentleman was pleasantly surprised and even displayed his sense of humour, "I had thought you to be deaf and mute as I do not recollect having spoken to you before. Come over to our place one of these days. It has always been either your mother or Rhea coming over to hand over the rent cheque."

Aryan acknowledged the invite with a smile to begin his day. He walked past his neighbourhood with a pleasant feeling of warmth and familiarity.

Out of an inexplicable impulse, he decided to take a bus to his college. Riding the bus, travelling through the city, Aryan looked at the teeming population invading the peak business hours with their merchandise. He felt left out of the organised chaos. He felt the desire to break free of the shackles that had prevented him from being a party to the chaos.

The desire had become invigorating within him. He got off the bus and walked briskly towards the college to be greeted with anonymity, very similar to his first day at the college. He shrugged off the tag of a stranger with a confident swagger and overheard young women talking at his back, "He must be a post-graduate senior. Look at the way he is stroking his hair, real handsome hunk."

The compliment from the women sent a sudden rush of adrenalin as he turned towards them in returning the compliment with a smile. It was more of a feeble attempt at disowning the troubled past of his uneventful life. This stage in life seemed to be holding the excitement of a promising tomorrow. He was consciously shedding his inhibitions while treading past the thresholds of the college to reconnect with himself.

He figured out the canteen, which was still wearing a lone look from outside. It was wearing dilapidated ornaments of plasters having come off at too many places. But once inside, the life was calling in the best of its attire of vigour, vibrancy and the unquestioned jubilation of carefree youth.

A very few bothered to cast a glance at the stranger, but he did turn a few heads among the women, secretly admiring the gait of a confident young man. Aryan swallowed the insignificance of yesteryears during his college days along with the tea and biscuits. He had made a point to himself. He had made his presence felt!

It was evening as Aryan was getting out of the house to take a stroll. Rhea made the first exclamation which sounded more of an admission, "You look different, bhaiya! Is it because you have tucked in your shirt or is it something else?"

Aryan blushed as he tried unabashedly to hide his embarrassment in his sheepish smile. "Aryan, you will meet the landlord to hand over the rent, tomorrow." That was his mother. A careful note would not have escaped the tears welling up in her eyes, to witness the blossoming of Aryan into a man.

Aryan climbed up the stairs to the first floor of the house. It was the first weekend of the month. He knocked the door which was ajar. Finding no one answering the knock, he pushed the door lightly, which led him to the living room. He stood still at the door and observed the living room, tastefully laid out with sparse furniture and fixtures and yet exuded the alluring warmth of playing an immaculate host. A lady peeped from the adjoining kitchen and waved at him to come inside, waking up Aryan from his trance. The lady had evidently rushed at working on herself while cooking, to look presentable before the guest.

She was magnificently pretty in her wheatish complexion, with her well-endowed curves in the right proportions, with the crowning glory being no less of opulence in curls, running up to her hips. She seemed to be aware of the desire that she could invoke in men and that made her more appealing. She walked up to Aryan with an air of nonchalance, her eyes fixed at him.

Aryan's throat was parched gasping for water, his palms were sweating, but he had his eyes fixed on her as well. Before his admiration turned into an unwelcome stare, he reclaimed his senses to hand out the envelope to her and made a brave attempt to break into a conversation which ended up as a coarse murmur, "Ma has sent the rent for the month."

"Does your mother still scold you, if you talk to strangers? I am Kavya. I have seen you off and on, lost in yourself. Please sit down and watch the IPL. My father-in-law must be on his way back from the evening walk. Let me get you a cup of tea or would you want a glass of water?" The lady tried to comfort Aryan.

The question was direct and sharp, as if she had seen him through his perversion. Aryan had plummeted onto the sofa by the time she returned with a glass of water. He got up in sheer disgust of soliciting courtesies from the lady in the absence of other members in the house. She smiled at him, sensing his discomfort. Kavya disarmed him of his chivalry as she handed him the glass of water. "You are a grown up man. As any other woman, I am gifted with a special sense to see through men and their intentions. You don't have to feel awkward in the absence of the other members of my family."

She touched him on his shoulders and seated him. "You do not have a friend, definitely not a friend who is a woman. I do not eat men for dinner."

Aryan felt assured, but was numb to respond to the digs taken at him, overpowered by the roving eyes of the woman! He was sure that his current state of being in a daze was the only chastity belt with which he was defending his temptations.

He felt defenseless as he misread the taunts to be the playfulness of the woman. He rose up from the sofa to put on his slippers when he heard the landlord walking up home. He stood still as the elderly gentleman came upstairs to greet him at the stairway. "Oh it is you, Aryan! When did you come?"

Before he could respond, the voice from inside answered, "He has been waiting for half an hour now to hand over the cheque to you. He hardly speaks, but day dreams a lot." She glanced at him, while ushering them inside the house.

Aryan was frantically looking for a place to hide his face. He realized that his hunch about Kavya was nothing more than an erotic association to an inert desire for a *woman;* who frequented his dream almost every other night, but only to ride away with someone else.

A man emerged from one of the rooms inside, clad in casual attire and greeted him, "I was taking a bath when

Kavya mentioned to me that you are here. I hope it is not for the job. Let's have another round of tea." It was Arvind!

Aryan looked at the mirror across the room to silently admonish himself. He had not even taken note of Arvind, during all these months that they had been staying with them as a tenant. The landlord and Kavya had every reason to take the digs at him.

He realized that he had become a narrow-minded man who salivated at the sight of any woman who came across him. It was unacceptable that women merely qualified for his wild inebriated fantasies. His remorse made him to be indignant with himself. Kavya came to the living room as she served tea to everyone with hot snacks and took another calculated jibe at him. "Aryan, you have no reason to be so undignified in your encounter with a woman who you meet for the first time." Kavya was reasonable and assertive when she spoke and it was difficult to not take cognizance of the conviction in her voice.

Arvind took control of the situation before it could spin out of control and comforted Aryan. "Growing up is similar to peeling an onion. It is a challenge to hold back the tears while peeling, but once you are done, you get the fleshy succulent onion. Similarly, the traits of a man need a dressing down in keeping the temptations at bay, to emerge a man of character. Some people call it the aura or personality, and I call it the intrinsic value that radiates around a real man." Arvind volunteered his take on the situation.

Aryan realized that deniability would land him nowhere and instead he must use the occasion to build upon a new relationship; something he had been longing for quite some time now. Kavya came up to the door to see him off and touched him by his shoulders. "You are no longer shivering with my touch. Please consider us to be your well-wishers and come to us whenever you need a friend to confide and share or need a shoulder to cry."

Aryan felt tears welling up his eyes while rushing downstairs, barely missing a few steps in his descent, but was in control of his emotions as he learnt that he could cry out of joy as well. He came to terms with the incident and accepted the fact that most men look at women with sheer wantonness, but men like Arvind are way too evolved in their outlook to treat and consider women at par. That made men of his likes so endearingly desirable to women.

Aryan had his dreams, but thankfully, he remained preoccupied with his self discovery in the pursuit of his happiness. In the morning, Kavya's presence at their place delighted him. She teased him in the presence of his sister. "Rhea, meet my new boyfriend. He is so unpretentious and sweet that even Arvind approves of him."

Aryan was still groggy but Kavya's giggles made him feel safe and dependable. "Aryan, go and meet this gentleman at the anchor store of the RGV mall. They are looking at employing someone like you as a floor assistant. He happens to be Arvind's friend and both of us feel that this could be a good start for your career." She tucked a paper to his hand. He took down the details and unassumingly thanked her.

The breakfast was ready and Kavya excused herself despite Rhea's insistence to accompany them at the table. Aryan noticed the intensity in his mother's eyes silently approving of a family time before Rhea could leave for her college and Aryan to try his luck with the job. "Aryan, be sure of one thing. You have been helped by Arvind to meet the gentleman, but the opportunity at the workplace is all about how you get to present your intensions to be engaged. Do not feel obligated towards Arvind, because you will land the job only if you are found deserving it." That was Kavya's parting shot!

Aryan got the job as the floor assistant with one of the most respected multi-brand stores at the RGV shopping mall. With a monthly salary of 15,000/- and other petty expenses to cover for the unearthly hours, the job was to handle interesting customers and their discretions and not to forget the cleaning of the mess and rearranging the trial rooms.

Aryan ticked another item in his checklist!

The mass communication course was an outstanding platform for Rhea to broad base her otherwise conservative outlook in life. She was considered to be reasonably balanced by her family in applying her independence and a sense of judgement on situations. Her reasoning was found to be largely unbiased because she had the uncanny ability to disassociate people from events and situations at hand, before placing her point of view.

This tremendous quality in her as a person was making her popular with the class and the faculty alike, as she found herself getting nominated to various prestigious assignments as field work with eminent journalists. She started taking keen interest with research-backed fact finding and started documenting the best of practices in print and electronic media for subsequent application in her career. The new-found frontiers with learning made her absorbent and eagerly receptive to the information universe which she validated with proper research before articulating any article to be considered as news.

Rhea was most comfortable with being her usual self with her family. But deep within her inner self, she was impatient to make a mark in her penchant for investigative journalism. Thus, despite the popularity that she enjoyed in the campus, she had her head placed firmly on her shoulders in navigating her way to success. She was already in the good books of the faculty and the mentors.

With the exposure she received during her field trips and internship, she was almost assured of a placement with a coveted media house. All that she had to ensure was an uninterrupted brilliance at fetching the best of academic scores. She was unfailing in the disposition of her duties towards her family and secretly admired Aryan's priority checklist while she had her own uncompromising agenda to settle a score with Raghav in wresting back their home.

It has been two years since Aryan lost his father. The man had left them behind with an unrequited love and tenderness, embroiled with misplaced perceptions as a husband and a father. Arvind and Kavya had become an extended family in these two years. The solemnizing of the death anniversary was an exercise of simplicity in affairs that was devoid of any rites and rituals getting performed. Rhea was busy helping her mother in wrapping up the affairs for the day while Aryan was animatedly discussing his work with Arvind when their attention was drawn to the door.

It was Rohan, and upon his arrival, it completed the family circle after two long years of being away from each other, but in the absence of the original man of the house. The reunion seemed a little awkward considering the occasion. Kavya took the initiative with making everyone feel at ease as she volunteered to introduce everyone to Rohan and then led her folks back to their home.

Rohan being the youngest among siblings was always showered with all the attention and affection. Affection and attention had manifested into a submission by the entire family to his whims and fancies. The young lad had grown up to be an adult with his tantrums getting over-zealously protected and complied with. The excuse that was offered by their mother was that he had missed his father who was always on tour while he was growing up.

Rohan had a fair share of his growing adulthood symptoms with disregard for everything and everyone that had gradually manifested into being a present day youth. He felt that the world had begun and would end with him. Sanity of decisions got overruled by the insanity of rebellion. The belief had paved the path for his avid self-belief that anything and everything was merely a toy! The world became his playground as any relationship that mattered became ordinarily dispensable to him.

The substitution effect for the father in the toys and his tantrums were the sincere ally to his sense of reasoning against the world. That had already sown the seed in him in becoming perilously gifted as naturally pretentious. He believed he was rich and became the apple in the eyes of his peers. They felt delightfully fortunate in the company of his impeccable traits and the gait of a suave young man who had just arrived to rule the world.

Reema was no exception to his charm as her beguiling semi-urban roots were more convinced that he was her man. He was the man with whom she would ride the bike every evening to the shopping mall to catch a movie and then slip in to the fabled urban jungle. It was akin to the reel life imitating real life, while the rest of the worries were just a pack of cards.

Their mother, who was battling her own insecurities, kept on obliging Rohan with an unabashed face-off with life. While she was fairly aware of the development at Rohan's end, she considered it wise to steer clear of justifying Rohan's misdeeds with his siblings. The act of remaining a self-effacing mother remained her strength to pull off a probable coup within the household that had long seized to be a family. Battle lines were drawn. It was either her way or the highway for anyone who had any reservation with Rohan's plundering his own life. So, when Rohan announced that Reema's parents were insisting on their marriage, it did not come as a surprise to his siblings.

Rhea pounced at him. "What do you exactly mean? Marriage, is it? And you are just out of your business school!" The exclamation was laced with definite sarcasm. "So, who is going to feed your wife and what about your responsibilities towards the family? All these two years, while pursuing studies, you have been having your wild ways and I will not be a bit surprised if Ma has been supporting your pursuits beyond your studies. Or have you already pawned your self-esteem to your prospective in-laws?"

Rohan had anticipated the situation as he rose up from the chair, walked up to his luggage and shoved up an envelope right across Rhea's inquisitive eyes. "I have a job with a leading telecom company and if you need some extra money, call me. I will be glad to pass on some extra bucks every month towards your sober pursuits." He forced himself out of the household.

And, there was this petrichor. It was drizzling outside!

Kavya was caught in the crossfire while re-entering the quarters along with Arvind with some snacks, sweets and tea for all of them as she looked at Rohan with her eyes pleading with him to stay back. Rohan shrugged off, putting his luggage down. "When do you want us to meet Reema's parents?" That was Aryan. The much-deserved relief was exchanged across the room along with the snacks and the tea.

None of the family did offer any further question to Aryan, but for Kavya, "Do we get to stay back to discuss the preparations for the marriage or it is only within the family?"

A smile from Aryan was the acknowledgement of and the answer to Kavya and Arvind's unquestioned role in their lives. Arvind went on to regale everyone with the anecdotes of his marriage, comforting Rhea's annoyance with the sudden turn of events. What followed during the next few weeks was nothing short of a cinema! The marriage was a matter of convenience between Rohan and Reema as they prepared to relocate from one way of life to another for their livelihood. Life, they thought, was a toy to them!

Kavya and Arvind had seamlessly assumed the self-appointed roles of being the face of the marriage. Both of them took charge right from the invitee list, to the budget, the ceremony and the farewell. The aroma of the entire affair was lingering in the leftovers. The dried flowers and stray cases of lost luggage were eventually balanced with the payment of bills and the cursory pledges to remain in touch among the friends and relatives. Life limped back to normal. Kavya became the heartthrob of every young and old with her never-complaining, ever-smiling multi-tasking skills. Aryan was not an exception to the fondness for her.

The day came when Rohan had to leave with Reema. "Would you not be with us, when we get back the house?" The mother's voice was flailing in anticipation of hearing a yes from Rohan, but being bruised at heart with her old war scars. She was battered time and again with her disappointments as she heard what she expected to hear from Rohan.

"Ma, we have a life and I have a career. I will send you money every month. You take care of yourself."

The unrepentant wave from Rohan as he rode away in the taxi along with Reema seemed like a brilliant ploy. It was to console and congratulate him on having escaped the drudgery of a damning life along with a widow and his siblings. Nobody was moved while wiping off the black fume from the taxi's exhaust, but for the mother, who wiped off her tears as well.

It had been two years since the democratic mandate for a populist government gave the people an executive that they deserved. Every move by the incumbent government was under scrutiny with the visual grandeur of change in uprooting every possible relic of the previous regime. The government's move to unearth the possibility of tainted trails of the previous government was being considered a sinister one by the detractors and the media alike and it was making daily headlines. Some people termed it as a trial by the media.

The followers of faith in the present government started gathering news that was being made available to them in the media. It was shaping their opinions on the debt-ridden affairs of the state and in the disinterest by the industry captains in putting up manufacturing units to generate employment. Even the Indian multinational companies were shying away from investing in the service sector.

In the meanwhile, Rhea graduated with flying colours and joined a leading media house as an investigative reporter to cover the political beat. She was raring to go and make a mark in her career. Aryan was still a fixture at the store as the floor assistant. He suffered frequent pangs of impatience in breaking free from offering the plastic smile and assistance to the customers at the store.

The phone calls from Rohan were luck by chance, although their mother still pinned her hopes that Rohan would be around when needed. She counted her perseverance with a bated breath with each passing day. The three of them started meeting infrequently during the days, save for the weekly holidays. It was Rhea who regaled the audience which also included Kavya, with her exploits in re-discovering the people, politicians and their ploys as a journalist.

"Have you noticed Arvind recently?" Rhea threw the question to no one in particular while having tea on a lazy Sunday afternoon. "He ignored me, while I was walking back home yesterday evening. Or, it could be simply my new way of looking at people wearing the investigative journalist's hat!"

"He seems to be preoccupied with his work as he is responsible enough to handle his life," answered back Aryan. "So, what's new at work?" As he walked up to wash his hands, he gestured to his mother. She went inside the adjoining room to come out with an envelope with wads of currency notes.

"This is something that Aryan has saved for you and had asked me to hand it over to you." Aryan's mother handed an envelope to Rhea.

"You actually thought of me and saved so much?" Rhea reached out to Aryan and hugged him. "I have been waiting for a day like this and I am going to shop till I drop. I am going over to the RGV mall this evening and you are going to come along with me as a customer to your store." Aryan hugged her back and kissed her forehead with a silent wish for her to be successful in life. He also silently wished for her determination and resolve, when the time was right and they were ready to get back their house from Raghav.

The siblings were getting ready for their shopping in the evening as the cell phone rang. It was a call from Rohan to their mother, but it was difficult to make any sense of the conversation as the lady was talking and responding in mono syllables. The moment she was over with the phone call, she plunged onto the chair. "Oh! Not again, Rohan cannot keep ruining our lives every time there is a faint hope of rejoicing." Rhea screamed at her mother.

Reema had left for her parent's place as they were having issues with each other for quite some time. Rohan's work required him to keep long hours at his office which has been a constant source of irritation for Reema. It eventually became a compatibility issue. Rohan had been complaining every now and then that Reema did not take care of the household. How it's a source of embarrassment for him to play host to his colleagues with an unkempt house and with Reema questioning every female colleague's proximity with him. The mother shared the development with Aryan and Rhea with a hesitation, which sounded more of a plea to do something about it.

Rohan and Reema had got married against the sermons of the elderly in both the families, to rather settle down with their respective careers and then consider marriage. The marriage took place during their courtship days, which began with Valentine's Day and culminated into a marriage. As predictable as it was, their relationship had fallen apart, to qualifying for absolute disharmony in compatibility, mutual respect and trust. The couple had fallen prey to the trickery and treacherous path of misplaced trust. The ordeal continued almost every day, which ended with violent verbal and physical abuses. It not only dented their relationship, but also created an irrevocably disturbed relationship.

Reema had finally left him in utter despair and in the lurch of solitary confinement. She did not realize that she had submitted to her husband's measured manoeuvre. It was the ploy that required Rohan to play with the precision of a seasoned actor in justifying his infidelity. He had already taken the refuge under the welcoming wings of a scornful woman and paraded their illicit relationship with refined aplomb. The showmanship was so creative in its deceit that even the families could not take umbrage of the tumultuous merriment of those two creatures of abject dishonour. Reema had become a toy for Rohan!

"I am not going to be a part of this discussion anymore. I have had enough of you and Rohan spoiling every bit of our lives. You are a control freak. You knew very well that Reema will never find it easy to substitute your unjustified pampering that you have been extending to your younger son. But you still went ahead with the consent for the marriage." Rhea was screaming at her mother as she continued.

"You had an evil wish lurking somewhere deep inside, which always wanted their marriage to fail so that you could escape this place to join Rohan in taking control of his life. You are such a failure as a mother or even as a wife maybe, that you find it normal to placate your role as a self-effacing woman. You knew all along that they were troubled and yet chose to keep it to yourself. Why come to us now?" Rhea was fuming as she blurted out.

"I have never uttered a word against any one of you ever and you construed it to be my weakness. It has always been either one of you or your lives. Be it your dead father who lived a life of abject failure, Aryan and his mediocrity or you with your indecisiveness. Has it ever occurred to anyone of you that I exist? So what if I have pinned my hopes on Rohan?" The mother's thundering caught both of them with shock and surprise. She spoke at length with a whimper in her voice, unsure of her justification, but definitely with the vengeance of a woman who had been wronged.

Aryan held Rhea to walk her to the room and made her lie in her bed. Rhea was sobbing and screaming at the same time. "Bhaiya, this cannot keep happening to me every time. Today was a day that I was looking forward to. I have my friends and colleagues who go out with their family and friends and I envied them. Today, when you gave me the money to shop and told me that you will be accompanying me, I was elated and then this happened." Rhea was pleading with Aryan.

"Stop crying for once and let me handle Ma for now," Aryan consoled her.

Aryan came back to their living room to find his mother's gaze fixed at him, which sent a chill down his spine. He did not remember seeing his mother as battle ready as she was, to confront all the odds that came in the way. Aryan sat beside her and offered her water and as he was about to speak; she raised her finger.

In an admonishing tone, she asked him to get Rhea along and hear her out. It was a monologue from the mother directed towards her children and they heard her out at length. It was the first time that the lady spoke with them with so much intensity and emotion that they had no other option but to sit beside her to listen to her life's share of agonies and ecstasy, if any.

"Do you remember visiting your grandparents on either side? You will not, because we have never taken you to either of them. I was born in a very wealthy family that had a flourishing business in the trading of commodities. I never knew how it felt to ask for something, as everything was made available to us and it was at our beck and call.

While at college, I met your father and fell for his rustic charm. He was a rebel at heart, poet with words and a champion of life. We got married immediately after your father landed his job after our studies, much to the chagrin and the wishes of our respective families. We had severed all our ties with the families as we walked out of them, never to be owned back again." Rhea made her mother to take a sip of the water as she spoke.

"But life had its share of reality check for us. Your father hailed from a reputed family of academicians whose principles were uncompromising to the point of unreasonable rigidity. At his work place, your father chose to be branded a rebel that led to his failure. He opposed all those practices that were considered unethical, but are largely accepted as the preamble of running a business." She was gradually gaining her composure while sharing her life story.

"Let me admit that it was a challenge to run a family of five, but your father never wanted to compromise on the quality of education for any one of you. I had chosen my life and had no other option but to concur with your father at the cost of substituting the life of a wife with that of a mother of three. But I was as vulnerable as any other woman of my age during my times and started missing out on the materialistic aspects of life. I had dreamt of a house of my own from where my children would be riding a car to their school and coming back to all the pleasantries, which a well-to-do family could offer. I envied women flaunting their heirloom, jewellery, clothes and their annual vacations.

"I was getting tired of a life in living each day as it came and gradually my wantonness took shape of a disinterested silence. I do not remember of a day discussing the tomorrow with your father, who seemed to be running away from fighting the same demons as me. Our lives became so predictably dreary that I had become a machine to outlive my age."

"After your father's death, when Rohan made it to the business school, I realized that somewhere my unrealised desires got a fresh lease of life. I wanted to reclaim those days that I had lost, but it made a demon out of me. I know I have ruined his life." She broke down miserably like a child, resting her head on Aryan's shoulders in remorse. "How do I redeem myself, Aryan? Please help me. I am tired of fighting these battles over the years and I remain lonely as ever."

Aryan helped his mother to walk up to her bed and as she slipped in it, Rhea rushed to throw herself at her. Aryan ran his fingers through his mother's hair while Rhea sang a song that she had heard her mother sing to her when she was a child. The roles were reversed as the daughter and the son put their mother to a peaceful sleep after endless nights of her having remained awake.

Occasional relief comes with the travesty to throw tantrums at sadness and disappointments. You relish happiness once in a while because too much of happiness too soon would have made it a drab affair! While the siblings were getting ready for their work, their mother was busy in the kitchen making a breakfast of their choice.

It was a refreshing morning that held a promise for a delightful day after having put aside the emotional upheavals of the previous night in a back burner. Aryan chose to turn a blind eye to Rhea's sense of guilt as she was being overtly affectionate with her mother. There was no reference to the revelations that were made the previous night, as the two of them put in extra efforts to make the togetherness. It looked a little too obvious for Aryan's impatience as he almost ran out of the house. He was at the gate when he noticed Kavya getting out of a taxi along with her father-in-law. It was late in the morning for a walk and he did not remember Kavya accompanying the old gentleman to his routine walk that he took every morning.

"Late for the morning walk?" quipped Aryan. "Where is Arvind?"

"Aryan, please wait as I walk my father-in-law upstairs. I need to speak to you."

There was a sense of urgency in Kavya's voice as Aryan looked at his watch. He did have some buffer to reach his workplace.

"I had come down to your place yesterday late evening, but sensing the frayed tempers flying around at your house, did not knock the door. Arvind came back this morning and claimed to have been at his office the entire night, as he had deadlines to meet. I am concerned about him as he is not his normal self these days. The zest is missing in his life as he remains pensive and lost somewhere, when he is at home. I do not know what to do with him as he is polite with his words but is aggrieved with something or someone, which he is not sharing with me."

"Kavya, you are my go-to person whenever I have faced any issue or crisis and now you come to me with your concern and I do not know how to react. It must be his work that's taking a toll on his peace of mind. Nevertheless, let me get to my work now and I will speak to him. Has there been any issue outside his work that you might know?"

"That is exactly what is bothering me so much. It has rarely happened that Arvind has not confided his problems with me. He is so detached with everyone these days." Kavya's voice was concerned and that was a rare.

"Let me come back and we will talk to him." Aryan patted her back reassuringly and left for his work.

Breaking News

The RGV Mall was an eloquent expression in indulgence from the very day it opened its doors to the public. In fact, it was difficult to accept that a shopping mall of such discerning taste could come from Raghav's stable; but then you have to give the actual credit to Priya who was the real brain behind putting up such an extravaganza. The best of the minds were put to work with a sharp eye for details.

Care was taken to ensure that the rich and the famous who holiday abroad but rue the fact that the city had nothing to offer, must find a reason to cheer back at home in flaunting the designer labels from GAP to Gucci. In other words, the RGV Mall was the newest reason to cheer, in the otherwise humdrum of the city life.

Aryan had worked up the ranks in the last three years in becoming the supervisor at the anchor store. Mentoring the trainees and guiding the regular shop floor attendants, he was the vigilant senior to make shopping a delightful experience at the store. The store was an ensemble of human emotions.

The tasks ranged from reasoning with the petite lady caught shoplifting to allaying the apprehensions of a bored housewife that the trial rooms had eyes! From anticipating the next move of the pot-bellied *nouveou riche* in abandoning the musk cologne in favour of a negligee for his consort, to politely helping the self-proclaimed celebrity in settling down with the right size for her rotund curvature.

Tucked in one of the corners of the lavish building was the plush office of the RGV Enterprises. It housed more than two hundred people overlooking various operations of the enterprise that ranged from real estate, hotels, print and prime time electronic media, educational institutions, steel and cement factories... if someone were to go by the claims made in their website. Although the rumours that did rounds within the mall and beyond, had an altogether different story to tell. The intelligentsia considered Raghav to be the conduit for many politicians and businessmen who had hoarded unaccounted money to find a safe haven in funding the epitaph of black money in the disguise of the shopping mall. The RGV Mall was essentially a pretense in creating a legal cover for their nefarious activities.

In the meanwhile, the change that ushered in at the political level made many people to sit up and start noticing that the needle has started to move! The politicians and their henchmen were convinced that the people who had voted for the change wanted a visible turnaround. The headlines were being made with the completion of the stalled projects along with the announcement of infrastructural and urban development plans. Socially relevant measures were getting implemented with the focus on rural education, health and parallely driving the popular theme of alleviating the girl child.

Raghav and Priya got featured prominently almost every day across press releases and electronic media and were hailed as the messiah of the masses! The political censorship went kaput as the ministers of the state were noticed hobnobbing with Raghav and his clan, at the stone-laying ceremonies of bridges, roads and factories. The conquest of the conundrum carried on and so did the life and times of people like Aryan, who had very little to complain in their fight for a daily living.

At the RGV Enterprises, Priya walked the corridors of uncontested power, being at the helm of affairs in representing the empire. Her office was embellished with an oak-bedecked desk, leather-bound high back chair and a whole host of gadgets which resembled nothing less than a war room.

Priya was in control of her commands in unleashing the meteoric rise of the conglomerate. She was irascible and rigid with her people, but pleasantly obliging with her patrons. She was rightly aware of the fact that her coveted position was destined to be a short stint, considering the company of the sycophants around her. It was difficult to fathom the prima donna beyond her high handedness with which she dispensed off her adversaries and the pretentious alike.

Aryan was just in time for the mall. The morning staffs across the outlets were seen busy with dressing the mannequins and merchandising the shelves. The housekeeping was leisurely mopping the floor with their eyes everywhere, but the floor. The malls' security personnel were duly attentive with their drill and details. The Labradors were unusually excited at the prospect of sniffing something different during the day when a bevy of straight-jacketed gentlemen walked into the mall, heading towards the RGV Mall's office.

"Priya madam has landed herself in a soup," quipped a guy while mopping the floor. In his almost juvenile candor, he murmured again, "Some government officials are raiding her office." Aryan took a look at him and he vanished from his sight.

The trainee who was beside Aryan volunteered a trivia. "This journalist Rhea seems to have drilled some sense at last!"

"Which reporter did you mention?" Aryan was caught unaware.

"You must have missed the headlines in the newspaper today. The young reporter in question is called Rhea, who has spilled the beans on RGV with the elaborate account of what goes behind the curtains." The guy was dismissive of Aryan's ignorance as he replied.

"Are you sure that the name of the journalist is Rhea?" asked Aryan, more in amazement and less in disbelief.

"That's what the newspaper says. She is now the darling of the people. Go ahead and check the newspaper for yourself, chief," the trainee grinned at him.

Aryan fished out his cell phone and rang up Rhea's number, which was not reachable, as was expected. He called up his mother's number, which got answered by Kavya. "Yes, it is true; our Rhea has shot into instant fame with her first assignment in investigative journalism." Kavya did not hide her admiration as she rattled off the narrative from the newspaper. Aryan was not sure how to react as he hung the phone to dash out of the mall to locate the nearest newspaper vendor.

It was 11.00 a.m., with all the roads leading to the mall choking with hundreds of onlookers as the government officials were seen dashing in and out of the mall building. Aryan was frantically looking for a newspaper, but realizing it was already late during the day for a vendor to be seen around, gave up his hope midway. The news sold like hot potatoes and after having made early gains, the vendors were already a party of the inquisitive onlookers in front of the mall. The policemen were seen taking guard as the cavalcade of the press started trooping at all vantage positions to beam the live telecast of one of the most anticipated revelations in many years. It involved the high and the mighty in their lust for money in having morphed the government and its machinery into redundancy.

In the chaos around and the ensuing melee between the police, press and the people, Aryan chanced upon Rhea, taking the flight of stairs to enter the mall with a band of followers towing her heels. They were the other reporters and photographer trying to extract the last pound of flesh as a mark of salvaging whatever was left to be their pride! It was incredibly gratifying for Aryan to witness his sister taking giant strides to steal the limelight from the veterans in the trade of '*breaking news*'.

There she was in front of Aryan, radiating in all her glory. "Rhea, you never mentioned this to us, even yesterday?" Aryan asked absolutely puzzled.

"Bhaiya, I am out of breath. Is it ok if we discuss this once I am at home?" Rhea vanished, leaving her brother baffled.

A visibly proud brother wanted to take her in his wings, but considering the inappropriateness of the situation, he patted her back and took a step aside to let her conclude the accomplishment. The outlets were hurriedly pulling down their shutters fearing a backlash from the irate and impatient mob, waiting to pounce upon anything and everything remotely associated with RGV Enterprise. Aryan felt a tuck at his elbow as he noticed a middle-aged man gesturing to follow him. Aryan's raised eyebrow was answered immediately.

"Priya madam wishes to see you right now. She has sent me to fetch you to her office. Please come along."

Sensing the impending trouble, Aryan was determined to escort Rhea back home, which however, seemed a remote possibility as she was nowhere to be seen in the vicinity. "Tell me where I have to go to see your Priya madam," assuring the man to keep his word, as he spoke to him while his eyes were looking for Rhea in the crowd.

"Madam is in her office and she has instructed me to take you to her."

"But I have to go to my store to check out the situation over there and then if I am available, I will go to see her at her office."

"As you wish, but I don't know how long she will be available in her office to meet you as the officials have started interrogating the top brass and she is next in the line of fire."

"Well then, I will come down as soon as possible." Aryan rushed to his store. The store was almost empty, but for the staff who looked worried and impatient for instructions. The store manager had organised a huddle to share the news that the store would remain closed till further advice from the management.

Aryan had all the time he could ask for, but it was his inquisitiveness that he made him run towards Priya's office. The office had turned into an impregnable ghetto with the policemen manning the entrance and frisking anyone who asked to go inside the office premises. Aryan found the middle-aged man who had gone to fetch him at the entrance, and before he could endure the cold gaze from the policemen and the strip tease that were to follow, he saw the man hurrying towards him.

"This gentleman is Rhea madam's elder brother," was all he had to say to make way for him by the policemen.

"Why did you utter Rhea's name?"

"Well, that was the easiest way to get you in without any hassle and was strictly in accordance with Priya madam's instructions. Incidentally, I am the whistleblower and was interviewed by your sister over the phone, before she decided to drop the bomb."

Somewhere deep within, Aryan sensed a concern for Rhea's well-being as the whistleblower whisked him off his feet to lead him to Priya's office. Rhea had taken the bull by its horns by plundering the very backyard and the bastion of Raghav's sinister designs. She must have endured a rough ride already, but hopefully, she was prepared for the face-off and its consequences. Or, was it merely a personal agenda that waited all these years? If the agenda stood settled with the unearthing of the scam that had led to Raghav's downfall, then Aryan had to admit that she had been singularly daunting and uncompromisingly fearless in her conquest.

Aryan noticed that the office was plagued with fear and uncertainty as the staff looked clueless and worried. These were the same people who till the other day were engrossed with duping the hapless and the uninitiated people of their hard-earned money in creating one of the biggest money market scams in the recent times. The hotels, factories, television channels and every other entity that were in the brochures of RGV Enterprises was nothing but a decoy to strip the thousands of investors to their last clothing and their livelihood.

There she was, the goddess herself! The turmoil had taken a toll on her otherwise impetuous demeanour that made her infamous, but she radiated a glow. There was definitely something about Priya which made her unattainable and yet very desirable. She rose up from her chair as she noticed Aryan entering her office. Unmindful of her gait, as she walked across the room to pull the blinds, Aryan poured himself a glass of water and drank it in a single breath. She gestured Aryan to take the seat in front of her as she gently rested herself in her chair. She was in for the occasion as she looked completely unperturbed with the turn of events.

The kohl-lined eyes must have seen the dreary days ahead of her. The face that lit a thousand lamps was devoid of any emotional upheaval. Her attire was sensuous in revealing her feline moves; leaving the detractors in her organisation fantasizing for an encounter in promiscuity from her, but of course, without a sense of guilt. In fact, that was the best moral judgment they could exercise against her stardom, whenever they got browbeaten by her astuteness. The eyelashes were the whip to bring back senses for anybody, who refused to kneel before her in abject servitude.

"How are you, Aryan?" she asked and without waiting for Aryan to respond, she went on. "I understand, you are in a dilemma and it makes sense, as no one would want to be seen with me now, in light of the recent developments."

Aryan retorted sharply. "It is not what you want me to think of you, madam!"

Priya batted her eyelashes. "Oh! When did I become a madam for you, Aryan?"

Aryan remained unmoved by her advances. "That's what everyone addresses you to be."

"But you are not among them. I remember your salivating at the prospect of courting an arm candy when you came for the styling class. I did not take any offence, because I was used to being considered an object of intense fantasy by men and you were not an exception to the rule," Priya lashed out at him.

"Why did you ask for me?" Aryan asked evading the direct assault.

"I have asked you to see me for two reasons. First of all, do compliment your sister Rhea on my behalf. I had discounted her as a novice who was looking for her break in her first few attempts at getting my time for an interview. Little did I realise that she would become the proverbial bee, which could sting!" Priya sounded menacing, which was nothing close to the complimenting voice that she wanted to convey to Rhea.

"However, I consider her work to be a non-event. I have no desire to elevate her to a stardom that she doesn't deserve right at this point, as she was doing her job and she did it pretty well for a starter," Priya continued with justifying her fallen status.

"So, you called me to issue a veiled threat to Rhea, now that the world knows the crook behind the pretty face?" Aryan shot back at her as a protective brother.

"Oh! Aryan, you are so gullible, for you relationships are important to you. Have you ever thought of yourself and your life ahead? Or, is it because you want to remain a hermit by renouncing your life for all the relationships, which you hold so dear to yourself?"

"And, why must it matter to you Priya?" At the face of her condescense, Aryan thundered at Priya with vigour, which he must have found for the first time in himself.

"It never mattered to you when you sold me the course and then left the styling school without even bothering about the people who you ended up duping. In your quest for the sky, you have grounded the dreams of so many people like me."

"I was doing my job!" It was a feeble whisper from Priya.

"You are so weak and dependent that you found the right cover in your arrogance to hide your cowardice in the veil of a shallow power that comes to you with the chair that you occupy." Aryan rose up from his chair, had his eyes fixed and fingers pointed at Priya as he spoke to her. Priya sank in her chair in absolute amazement.

"Go on Aryan, I am meeting a man who can give it back to me after a long time."

"Your bitterness has made you self-destructive. You can at best be an arm candy to a man and nothing else." Aryan sounded empathetic.

"Now that you had your say Aryan, let me tell you something." It was Priya's turn to present her side of the story. "When I look at men, you are no more than beasts in waiting, ready to pounce at any woman any time. You are conditioned to look at us as temptresses and performers who will moan and give deep throated grunts, while you are about to finish your act. And then, when you zip up your trousers, you expect us to immerse you in adulation for your performance, which never took place."

"I did not come to listen to the crass acts, which you must be staging with every other man. Now, tell me what exactly is the reason behind seeing me? Get over with your acts and mind it, Rhea is not alone; she has a brother to take care of her." Aryan was getting ready for the door.

"Aryan, please sit down. I have very little time left to amend certain very important things." Priya sighed as Aryan turned around and sat down while exercising a measured caution against what would come next from her.

"My life during the last thrity-five years has been eventful enough to teach me a lot of lessons. I do not hold anyone responsible for wherever I have landed myself today. It has been an indulgence with my own life. I did not ask you to meet me to issue any veiled threat for Rhea, but to request you to flee this flea market and start your career afresh. I am aware that you are committed to your family first." Aryan was in for a shock, hearing Priya's plea with him.

"Have you been stalking me all this while? What is your interest in me and my family?" Aryan asked with all sincerity.

"Aryan, the revelation involves two families. I have spoken to Aesthetics; they owe me a lot in favour. They are more than keen to take you as one of their stylists at their master outlet."

There was a knock at the door as one of the office assistants interrupted. "Madam, the officers are looking for you".

"Tell them, I will be with them shortly." Priya turned around to Aryan and went on. "Arvind used to work for us, unofficially. He used the database of his bank to promote and sell our time deposits. He wanted to make a lot of money, really fast. And thus, he chose to make the best use of the opportunity that we offered him. He was not the only one, though, to have fallen prey to the primitive vice of greed."

"Where is Arvind? He is not his normal self and his wife is worried," Aryan asked with concern.

"He must be already into hiding somewhere. It was Arvind who shared your might to fight the plight of today to emerge victorious tomorrow! I hold nothing against Rhea and I will be happy for you and your family when you get the rightful due from Raghav." Priya looked unfailingly human with her admissions making her vulnerable enough to look for a shoulder and cry.

Aryan rose up from his chair and looked at her. She was cowering for a cover and despite all her brave acts of fooling herself to chase her ambitions, she was crestfallen. If these were the outcome of success, Aryan was happy with whatever he had for himself.

Priya got up to see off Aryan to the door and just as he was to hold the door knob, she held his hand. Priya had tears in her eyes as she spoke, "Aryan, I am done for good. You stay blessed and conquer your dreams." She embraced Aryan in a tight hug as he held her in his arms. While she caressed his hair, Aryan kissed her forehead, absolutely unsure of what made him do that. "Thank you Aryan. If the paths ever cross our lives, I would be delighted to meet the gentleman that you are."

Aryan remained speechless as he freed himself from Priya to walk out of the dungeons of despair at the RGV Enterprises. As he walked out, he noticed Rhea, immersed in her conversations with the officials. Rhea was going to be the headlines for some more days to come, as Aryan let her be with herself, to come out in the open air outside the RGV mall.

Aryan's house was on the ground floor with a meandering garden by the path leading to their door. The garden was in full bloom, thanks to the untiring attendance by their landlord. The whiffs of the seasonal flowers had a soothing effect on the frayed nerves of someone crossing the garden. Aryan did not catch the fragrance as he stopped by to take a look at the flowers. Nothing was unusual with the flowers, but it surely did not emit any fragrance that day, something that he was used to, while walking past them on any other day.

He came home early for the day, and unannounced. Expecting his mother to be in the kitchen, he wanted to spring a surprise, but she was nowhere to be seen. He came out of the kitchen and chanced upon the newspaper and smiled by himself while neatly folding the paper and placing it back at the table. He came out of their house and saw her mother climbing down the stairs from the first floor. She must have heard him coming.

"What happened to you Ma? You look worried, and by the way, you did not mention Rhea's article in the newspaper while I was on my way to the store. She is the talk of the town. Ma! Rhea has nailed Raghav single-handedly and I have witnessed his empire crumbling down today," Aryan spoke all at once.

"Arvind's father had a cardiac arrest in the afternoon and he had to be taken to the hospital. There was no one at home and I accompanied Kavya. We returned a little while ago." His mother updated him.

"How is he? Is he out of danger?" Aryan enquired.

"How would I know, but I overheard the doctors asking Kavya to wait for the next seventy-two hours before they get to decide the next course of action. The poor woman had to do everything in Arvind's absence. How come he has suddenly turned so irresponsible?" complained his mother.

"Ma, he is a result of the circumstances that he forced upon himself and all it will take is some time and a lesson from life; before he comes back as the same old reliable Arvind that he is known to us. Let me go and meet Kavya for now." Aryan dashed upstairs, barely finishing his sentence.

Kavya was absentmindedly staring at the walls with a cup of tea held in her hands when she regained her senses. Aryan went up to her, calling out her name, enquiring about her father-in-law. "My sixth sense has been telling me that something was terribly wrong with Arvind and I do not think the old man is going to survive the treachery inflicted by his son." Kavya was calm as she spoke and gestured Aryan to sit beside her in the sofa.

"What do you mean?" asked Aryan.

"I received an envelope from Arvind's bank yesterday, and thinking there must be something that requires a response, called up his number. He was not reachable and I was growing restless in his absence. My father-in-law had noticed it and he volunteered to open the envelope marked for Arvind. He read the content, and without sharing anything with me, retired to his room. He suffered the cardiac arrest this morning, presumably after reading the content which must have left him with no choice," Kavya gave a detailed reply.

"But what was written in the letter?" asked Aryan.

"Arvind has been terminated from his job at the bank with immediate effect for breach of trust and client confidentiality agreement. The bank is considering filing for criminal charges, for which he has been show caused. It is so difficult to accept that Arvind would have committed something so heinous." Kavya started sobbing as she continued, "All of you spoke so highly of him being such a thoroughbred man with uncompromising principles. Who do you think must have conspired to land him in this trouble?"

"Calm down, Kavya. I am sure Arvind has his own reasons to remain silent, but whatever little that I know of him, I expect him to surface very soon with his own admissions at an appropriate time," Aryan tried to reason out, but in vain, as Kavya was uncontrollable in her righteous offensive.

"What about his father? The old man has been my single support against the tirade, early in my marriage, hurled by Arvind's family members, including his mother. Has it ever occurred to you that we still remain a childless couple, in the ten years of our marriage? We have been saving money to treat Arvind's infertility as he wants a biological child. He has been a loving husband, giving me no reason to complain. I am actually disappointed, for he is a coward. He has broken the trust and respect in our marriage. He should have confided

in me, and we would have faced the situation as a couple."
Kavya broke down!

Aryan tried to comfort her with words that got eschewed
midway as Kavya got up from the sofa and took a glass of
water to sober down. She looked defiantly ravishing, even in
her dismay, as Aryan cursed himself for his insensitivity to
the occasion.

"What is the point in discussing all this in Arvind's
absence? Why don't we discuss it at some other time? Let's
rather get ready to visit your father-in-law at the hospital
and check out the formalities. And yes, do we carry some
cash?" Aryan was in no mood to discuss Kavya's marital life,
especially when he was privy to what had transpired of Arvind
and thus chose to divert the discomfort of the conversation
that was taking place.

Kavya looked at Aryan admiringly but stopped short at
saying anything to him as she paused to wipe off her cheeks
and then suddenly burst into laughter. It was possibly to hide
her embarrassment from Aryan. "Thank you, boyfriend, I am
feeling a lot lighter now. Would you mind waiting downstairs
while a lady gets ready?" She had reclaimed her senses!

Aryan was relieved that Kavya was coming back to her
old self as he walked towards their house on the ground
floor. His mother was waiting for him as she volunteered
help for Kavya. "Aryan, she might be needing money for the
hospitalization, let me know if we can be of some help."

Since Aryan was informed that they had saved money for
Arvind's treatment, he told his mother that he would check

back with Kavya to come back if she required any money for the treatment.

"Come back as soon as you are through with the hospital. I will be waiting for you, along with Rhea over dinner." That was the restless mother, zealously possessive of his son venturing out with another woman.

"Ma, I will ask Kavya to join us for dinner; she is all by herself," Aryan replied as he walked out of the house, hearing Kavya calling out to him. Aryan noticed his mother exchanging a forced smile with Kavya while her eyes pleading her son to be back under her wings. Understanding women had never been his forte, but of late, he seemed to be taking baby steps at it!

"Why are you smiling?" Kavya asked, as she hailed a cab.

"Nothing in particular, but the day has been riddled with so many intriguing events. I am smiling at myself at having handled each one of them, almost close to perfection!"

At the hospital, they were in at the rush time of the visiting hours and thus missed out the opportunity in observing the people and their exclamations. They would have otherwise mastered the art of reading people merely by their eyebrow movements depicting anxiety, anguish, detachment or the fear of the impending news waiting to be broken.

Arvind's father did not make it out of the life support system. Once they completed the formalities of at the hospital, Aryan & Kavya hired the hearse and went to the crematorium to complete the last rites. Arvind was nowhere to be found and his phone was not reachable. It was a sense of déjà vu for Aryan, but for the fact that the old man at the pyre was a father to someone else, who had chosen to remain out of the reach from his family.

"Aryan, will you have a coffee with me?" Kavya asked to break the imposing silence.

"I must get back home as Ma will be waiting for me to join her over dinner. You are joining us," Aryan replied to her.

"So, I was right when I told you that your mother still scolds you for talking to a stranger." Kavya giggled.

"That's not fair. There is a lot to be worked upon back at home, and I am eager to meet Rhea."

Kavya made no further fuss and tagged along with Aryan towards home, giving the coffee a miss for then.

Nature lends itself the unpredictability of its many moods through the elementary forms, but in myriad hues. The sky was overcast with the clouds flying by. It looked gloomy and overbearing, which reflected the state of affairs in the extended household of the landlord and their tenants. Aryan stopped at the garden after entering through the gate along with Kavya. He was looking for the fragrance that the flowers emit every day, but it was nowhere to be found.

"Aryan, the flowers are grieving and it seems they knew well ahead in advance that the old man will not walk back to his life. They were unattended since the last few days." Kavya echoed his thoughts as Aryan cuddled the shrubs one after another while walking back home.

"One of us must start attending to them, as life will go on as usual and I am pretty impatient to get a whiff of the life in these flowers," Aryan replied.

The clouds made a pass at them with a series of thunder, agreeing with the fact that life went on with or without the ones who you love.

"You go back to your mother and I will join you later at dinner." Kavya hurried towards the staircase.

"Kavya, do not attempt to be brave without a reason. Most certainly not for those reasons, that is not in your control. You will find the answers to all your questions and it requires you to be patient." Aryan sounded wise to his surprise.

"You sound so different. You seem to have grown up overnight, Aryan!" Kavya stopped midway, ascending the stairs.

"I have a choice to be different or to be definite and I choose to be definite with you, Kavya," Aryan added to her pleasant surprise.

"You go ahead while I try to come to terms with my life. But, does your mother approve of my joining you over at dinner? She still thinks that I eat men for dinner and you are a grown-up man now!" Kavya laughed aloud while holding back to hear out Aryan.

"Kavya, this is an age-old conflict between a mother and a woman. I think she is well within her rights to think and act as a mother, but she is not necessarily right when she thinks and acts as a woman. The onus is with you to dispel the myth surrounding you as the other woman, to win over her." Aryan summed up his sermon and served it quite well.

Kavya's voice sank almost to a whisper as Aryan was about to step towards their door on the ground floor, "Aryan, I am either a hapless victim of the present circumstances or I am helplessly falling for your charm." There was no pretence in her voice as she walked upstairs.

Aryan entered the house and found her mother mending some old rags, which was an annual exercise that the lady had been following for so many years now without a fail. She gathered old and unused clothes and meticulously worked upon them to make almost a new set of clothes. She distributed them among those who were in need of the clothes during the festive season. Durga Puja was a month around the corner and she was occupied with her avocation.

"Ma, I am back from the crematorium. Arvind's father breathed his last and we completed the rituals. Where is Rhea?" Aryan interrupted his mother who took her eyes from the intricate work, kept them aside carefully, looked at the wall clock and rose up from the floor.

"She had called up to inform that she will be late and asked me not to wait for her. Kavya might not feel comfortable in her absence. Why don't you freshen up while I carry the dinner up to her; she is in mourning and I am not sure if she will be comfortable eating with us. God bless the departed soul of Arvind's father." She had accepted the demise.

"I fail to understand something. You accompanied her to the hospital and then stayed with her till I returned home. You even enquired if she will need money for the hospitalization. Then you are suddenly choosing to cast away from her when she needs us?" Aryan took a stand against the derision that his mother was showing towards Kavya.

"I have my own reasons and I expect you to remain out of it. I have heard a lot about her from the women who I meet at the temple premises in the evenings. She is known to be a home-breaker, always found flirting with men. This had led to a huge issue with their previous tenant who was left with no choice but to vacate the house and save their marriage."

"This is just hearsay from some of the gossipmongers at the temple, Ma." Aryan's attempt to defend Kavya fell on deaf ears as his mother continued with her concerns.

"Aryan, she is married for the last ten years and they do not have a single child. It is her frivolous ways with life and the unacceptable conduct with men that has landed her in the present state."

Hearing all the slander being hurled at her, Aryan could not help but narrate the events of the day and the conversations that he separately had with Priya and with Kavya. "She is childlike and outgoing, but she is a woman of strong will. Did you ever come across any complaints from her father-in-law? Now that you know the reason behind Arvind's disappearance, I think we must extend our moral support to Kavya."

Aryan's mother was completely startled with the revelation and she gathered her wits to look out for Kavya. There she was, clinging on to the curtains. She was looking at Aryan's mother who had by then put up a disarming smile so that she could avoid the embarrassment. Kavya walked slowly to come and stand just in front of her. Aryan was dwarfed by the sudden development and started looking for a cue to escape the situation. He was shocked as Kavya broke into laughter with tears running down her cheeks.

She stopped laughing as she spoke out. "Relationships are cobwebs and when you try to break free, you get pulled back because of the sticky mess. Those who decisively remain in the web feast on the prey. Some of us are more fortunate to wriggle out of the cobweb, but again run the risk to come under a slipper. But if you can survive the slipper, you start to spin your own web. And, the relationships continue along with your life."

"Kavya, the elderly women at the temple have ruined Ma's sense of judgement. Those were not her opinions at all." Aryan defended his mother, which was more of a compulsive reaction to Kavya's invisible slap across his mother's face.

"Aryan, I did not ever consider breaking free of the cobweb of my life with Arvind, as I was happy in my own way. But now that I know what is keeping Arvind away from me, I will have to spin a web of my own, as I do not want those women to point their finger at me again. They are those slippers and I have to outwit them."

Aryan's mother could not take the outpourings of an embittered heart any longer as she took Kavya in her arms and tried to pacify the situation. "We will have dinner together. We will eat together every day, till Arvind returns."

She was not prepared for Kavya's tryst with a new resolve as she withdrew herself from the embrace. "You may not forgive me for saying this, but I want a life of my own. Arvind's return or no return is a nonevent. Let me tell you something, Arvind is as impotent in our relationship as he is medically infertile!"

The television set came back to life, screaming *breaking news*! Aryan's mother excused herself to the kitchen while Kavya sat down. Aryan was fiddling with the remote control to take refuge in his unsparing ways to escape Kavya's wrath, but instead he found her sitting relaxed on the sofa. She asked Aryan to increase the volume of the news channel. It was the most popular news channel, broadcasting the fallout of the RGV Enterprise scam. The channel was showing teasers in asking the viewers to stay back for the primetime talk show which was going to feature the journalist who had unearthed the scam and uprooted the myth surrounding RGV.

"They are going to have Rhea in the primetime talk show. Ma, you want to watch your daughter on TV? Come fast and join us. Dinner can wait for some time." Aryan almost screamed at the top of his voice in sheer excitement and joy.

Kavya joined them by inviting his mother to sit beside her, to watch the action live. "The girl did not let us have an inkling of the enormity of the task that she undertook. It is similar to befalling the grand trunk of the biggest banyan tree!"

Life went on as usual from the next day. The curious neighbours occasionally invaded in attempting at fishing for juicy gossip beyond what they learnt from the newspapers and the news channels. Rhea was indeed the toast of the times as she earned her prominence in the national media as well. She started getting featured now and then, with her share of opinion on the state of affairs. Rhea was hardly found at home as she had started to travel to New Delhi quite often.

Aryan had an intuition and it told him that Rhea would make it bigger, which would require shifting her base to New Delhi, the epicenter of all the things big and bright. Kavya was already at ease with the situation that she was in and found herself spending more time with the elderly lady. She had undergone a transformation with her acceptance for Kavya.

Aryan kept visiting the mall almost every day to find out what was in his fate and with that of others at the store. He was greeted with the notice that the store would remain closed till further advice. He was more than convinced that he had to work out an alternative at the earliest. Aryan started mulling the parting advice from Priya of joining Aesthetics as a stylist and decided to talk it out with Kavya and Rhea.

Kavya was busy helping Aryan's mother in the kitchen when he chanced upon her. They were discussing something with a lot of excitement between themselves. Guessing it to be a matter around Rhea's conquest, Aryan casually asked, "So, anything new with the news around"?

"We are planning to start a business out of our kitchen," his mother responded to the query and looked at Kavya admiringly. "It is Kavya's plan and we are working out the details."

Aryan was already keen. "And, what exactly do you propose to offer?"

"Look at the people around you. They all are running to fend for themselves and losing out in living a life in the bargain. They are missing out on what they grew up with and we plan to capitalize on their loss by offering homemade delicacies." That was Kavya at her pompous best.

"It is already sounding interesting enough to seek employment in your enterprise Kavya, now that I am unemployed." Aryan breached the zone of his own discomfort to raise the topic of checking out the prospect as a stylist at the Aesthetics.

"I do not see any reason why you should not. Besides, I do not see your adding any value in our enterprise." Kavya shared her opinion but did not spare him with the harmless tease as if Aryan was taking their plans lightly!

"Aryan, I do not think you father ever disapproved of pursuing a career of your choice. He wanted you to be decisive and steady, and if you have asked this question to seek my approval, you had it from the very beginning when you wanted to join the course," the mother had her say and it was such a relief for Aryan, as he left them with their plans.

It was late in the evening and Rhea was back at home, but she looked at little baffled, unlike her recent self. Aryan was observing her as she came to the living room. Rhea was silent, but one could make out that she was going through some turbulence. She held the saucer while sipping her tea and was vacantly looking at the television which was playing one of her own stories on Raghav and Priya.

"What is it, Rhea?" Aryan enquired.

"I am in a fix, bhaiya. I have been offered a role in news production with one of the biggest television channels," Rhea answered Aryan, but she was still unmindful.

"And, that will require you to move to New Delhi and you are worried about us? When do you have to move?" Aryan's calm demeanour while talking to his sister had the solution that she was looking for and tears of joy trickled down her checks.

"You are incredible, bhaiya. Yes, I am worried that you will be left alone with Ma and thus, I was in two minds," Rhea spoke sheepishly.

"Let's break the news to Ma and Kavya to get going with it."

Rhea tugged. While they were happy with the development, their mother looked a little grim beyond her pride for her daughter. They had a hearty mealtime as Aryan and Rhea took delightful digs into the food, complimenting their mother and Kavya of the impending success of their food venture.

"There's many a slip between the cup and the lip. Let the venture get to see the light of the day. I am actually wary of any good news that comes in this family." Rhea and Kavya exchanged disapproving glances with what the lady had to offer in lieu of a dessert for dinner. Aryan maintained a stony silence as he knew that it was something to do with Rohan!

At the dead of the night, the trembling voice of his mother woke him up with the phone in her hand, "Your brother is being taken into police custody. He was in Kolkata all this while and he had told us nothing about it."

The penny dropped for Aryan on the conversation that took place during their dinner. Bewildered, Aryan wasted no time in slipping out of his pyjamas to put on some clothes and rushed to the police station.

The investigating officer narrated the reason for his arrest with the finesse of an adept storyteller. Occasionally, taking liberty of the creative punches, as the narrative in itself was so gruesome in its facts that any other form of storytelling would have had to be factual enough to be considered as a work of art.

Rohan went after the other woman when Reema left him. The woman had already taken pity to his plight of being a neglected husband. Rohan had spun the fabric of cinematic chivalry as she took fancy to his earnestness of appeal. The other woman in question had already started dreaming of settling down unchallenged and triumphant in her chase of a travesty of promises made by Rohan. Interestingly, he was already embroiled in a legal battle with Reema on the grounds of domestic violence. He had managed to come out unscathed in striking a balanced account between his cheating of Reema and scripting his extramarital affair.

Anguish and dishonour took a new form for Aryan in his pleading with the police officer for a way out. There were plenty that could be preordained in forging accepted ways of resolving critical situations. The investigating officer was a veteran in suggesting a way out of the mess with an air of authority. It was very similar to the act of your family priest, who you find chanting verses in invoking celestial intervention to disrobe you out of your last clothes as an offering to ward off the evil eyes befallen. The investigating officer confided in Aryan of his proximity to the other woman and her family. He convinced Aryan to meet her in pacifying her frayed tempers, and in making an offer for an out of the court settlement.

Where did the question for a settlement arise? Well, the allegations against Rohan were that of the breach of trust and cheating which were cognizable offences that could land him behind bars. Aryan chose to play to the tunes of the *Pied Piper* to meet the other woman. The woman was forthcoming in her choice of carefully selected abuse for Rohan, who had played truant to her dreams of togetherness in suddenly taking a U-turn to get back to Reema.

After having crafted a script of separation with his wife and parading her as the other woman, how could she accept the breach of trust of having been promised a marriage? In their macabre sport of claiming love for each other, they had already gone ahead and made bold disclosure of their intentions with mutual friends and the woman's family. The woman claimed that Aryan's mother was privy to the same, who was repeatedly insisting them to not take their illicit relationship any further. Not till Rohan was still married to Reema and had not been legally granted a divorce.

Rohan and the woman went about unhindered in their exploits against all forms of societal bindings in throwing lavish parties and blowing money in togetherness. The celebrations were euphoric, but it started to form the roots for an impending disaster. The woman was in no hurry to reconcile to the not-so-well-thought-out apologies, either from Rohan, or from his family.

Aryan was considerably influenced by her narrative, but decided to stand out of the contemptuous situation. He came out of the police station, but not before taking a look at the custody. There he stood, behind the bars, caught with his pants down along with his pride. Looking like a wolf in a sheep's clothing, seeking refuge with empathy and yet unrepentant to his wild pursuits. *Rohan was behind the bars!*

The governance in the state was gathering momentum everyday with their empowerment policies. The opposition was vocal in terming them to be nothing more than appeasing the voters. The government got almost fanatical with vote bank politics while the opposition started gaining grounds to rework their strategies around the debt-ridden condition of the state exchequer.

The pitiful condition got reflected in the affairs around RGV Mall as well. The once formidable place that invited its patrons to indulge was decadent and it became a sore to the eyes of the beholders. The mall was a rhapsody by itself, synonymous to representing the corrupt, ruling the roost of the society and thus had become the symbol of a curse inflicted upon an act of rapacious greed. The perpetrators were at large.

The media kept reminding how those inglorious representatives of people kept their own interests safeguarded, under the patronage of the rich and powerful coteries. The same media that had helped the present government come to power were proving to be their nemesis.

Meanwhile, the people who had lost their money to the scandal were getting herded by the opposition to the government as a grim reminder to the fact that there was no respite from the tentacles of political tricks. The empathizers lost no time in shoving the issue under the carpet of judicial commissions. They got busy to work out gainful political equations and compromising formulas to make the best out of the political compulsions of the situation. *Birds of the same feather had to flock together*!

The mall remained unkempt and unattended. Almost all the outlets had closed down, prematurely. Those with deep pockets braved the heat to resume their businesses at a different address. The anchor store that employed the likes of Aryan turned a blind eye to them and the business prospects elsewhere, by deciding to pull down their shutters forever.

Aryan received the official confirmation of the outlet's closure at the mall along with the termination letter. The letter referred to the adverse business conditions being responsible for the unplanned retrenchment. Thankfully, his employer had sent the separation compensation along with a consolatory pay cheque for three months. That was the end of a chapter, but the beginning of a fresh lease of life for Aryan, who had by then decided to go ahead with trying his hands on scissors and combs.

It was the end of September as the mild chill in the air outside was romancing with the shorter stint of the sun rays. The feeling around the family, with what had taken place with Rohan, was similar to the dusk outside. It was dark outside! The family knew that they could do nothing about it. Durga Puja was around the corner and Rhea was getting ready to leave her family back at Kolkata for the unknown shores to strike it rich. Aryan and his mother were helping Rhea with packing her luggage while Kavya was attending the kitchen.

"I am taking the evening flight and I hope you guys are not packing my dinner." Rhea was somber in her mockery for Kavya's fondness with holding the fort in the kitchen.

"I have never flown till date, so how would I know what it takes to have the wings? I am happy remaining grounded till you send me flight tickets to join you at New Delhi." Kavya smiled at Rhea, without making any attempt to hide her resentment.

"Any news about Arvind? I wish we knew of his whereabouts before I left home." The darts were out as Rhea threw one at Kavya.

"How does it matter, Rhea? He must have buried himself in a pile of misery and remorse." Kavya avoided the piercing dart of the inquiry with a controlled but cold rebuttal.

"I don't have to remind you that you will be all by yourself and thus you have to be more careful with what you say and to whom you say. Your journalistic digs have already created enough trouble for all of us." The typical mother hen still had her daughter under her protective wings.

"Ma, all is not over yet. I will be just two hours of flying time from you and my work will keep bringing me here, now and then," Rhea comforted her mother.

"It is time for an early meal, everyone," Kavya interrupted them as she laid the plates and invited all of them to the table.

"I know you are cross with me. I should have avoided discussing Arvind. Actually, everything happened in such a jiffy that I seem to have lost balance. I am sorry." Rhea was apologetic as she hugged Kavya.

"The hug does not give you the respite from not sending the flight tickets." Kavya hugged her back and lightened the otherwise solemn mood around. The family was having their meal over casual conversations, which centered on the proposed food venture, carefully avoiding contentious issues any further.

"Rhea, once you are in Delhi, find out a bureaucrat's son and settle down with marriage." Kavya remarked giggling at her.

"I will hardly have time for such frivolous matters. I will have to make a mark for myself in a jungle where the rule of survival is all about making headlines and breaking news." Rhea sounded assertive with her purpose.

"Let Aryan find a stable job and then we can think of Rhea's marriage," the mother interjected.

"Ma, let Rhea settle down in Delhi and then we will have to think of something for Rohan. I do not have any bit of a clue as to how we go forward from here." Aryan was cold in his demeanour and that put an end to all the careless banter. They went about finishing their meal without any further ado.

It was a little after the early lunch when the family was relaxing on the couch and conducting the last-minute check on Rhea's packing when the phone rang. It was Reema, who was on the other side of the phone as Aryan gathered himself to talk to her.

"Yes Reema, what is it about?"

"Rohan has been sentenced to jail for two years, bhaiya."

"Can we talk a little later?"

"There is nothing to talk on this, bhaiya. I am the one to be blamed. I wish we had paid heed to all the advices that came from you all when you had asked us to focus on our careers before rushing into marriage." Reema was sobbing at the other end of the phone.

"Rhea is leaving for Delhi in a few hours from now. Is it okay if we get to talk sometime later in the evening?" Aryan wanted to pacify Reema who had disconnected the phone by then.

With the exchange of some furtive glances between all the four people in the room, everyone accepted the predictable phone call, which was bound to come some day or the other.

"Bhaiya, if I were in your place, I would not have pursued Rohan's case any further. He got what he deserved." Rhea was stunningly indifferent with her remarks.

"So, when do we leave for the airport?" Aryan enquired as he shrugged off Rhea's insensitivity for the occasion, in the presence of their mother. The lady went inside her room as Kavya walked off to her place without any further exchange of words.

"Bhaiya, I will be taking the 7.30 p.m. flight. You do not have to come along with me. Be with Ma. I can take care of myself," Rhea replied.

"You really have grown wings, Rhea. Big and strong enough to fly all by yourself." Aryan smiled at her.

"Not for anything, bhaiya. I have reached wherever I am today with my own ability." Rhea left the room.

Pride tasted a little bitter as Aryan felt an unfamiliar air of arrogance in Rhea. "So be it then. Be happy with your pursuits," Aryan murmured with no one around in the living room as he curled himself on the couch.

Aryan must have dozed off when he was woken up by Kavya with a cup of tea in her hands. "Wake up Aryan, Rhea is ready to leave."

Aryan was still drowsy as he went to the wash room to splash some water. He quickly put on some clothes and came out.

The cab was at the door and Rhea was ready to live her dreams. "I have not forgotten our checklist, bhaiya. We will get back our house from Raghav." She waved at all of them and the cab vanished in the busy street.

It was close to 10.30 p.m. when Aryan received the call from Rhea, informing him of her safe landing. She would be putting up at the company's guesthouse before she found a place for herself. It was late for them to have their dinner, but considering the fact that they were anxious of Rhea's phone call informing them of her reaching New Delhi, the departure from a routine did not occur as anything unusual. Kavya had retired to her place upstairs by then and it was only the duo of the mother and the son dining silently.

Aryan picked up his phone to dial Reema's number. She responded to his calls after a couple of rings. "Reema, I could not speak to you properly as all of us were occupied with helping Rhea pack her luggage."

"It is okay with me, bhaiya. Now that Rohan has to serve his two years term in jail, I have to start once again with my career. I don't think he is to be singularly blamed for the current situation that we are in, as I too have failed him as his wife," Reema sounded quite steady with her resolve and a little older than her age.

"I don't think so. You were batch-mates and you had your own career aspirations. Don't lose heart and keep trying and I am sure something will definitely work out in your favour. I wish I could help, but for the fact that I am in the same boat as you are." Aryan lent his support to Reema's determination to create an identity for herself.

"Thank you, bhaiya. You take care of yourself and I will keep you posted of developments at my end. Take care of Ma and tell her that I am sorry."

The entire conversation between Aryan and Reema was a sincere reinforcement of the relationship that was lost out on various counts. Both of them agreed that their relationship deserved an acknowledgement, that they would be there for each other when it mattered.

Aryan woke up in the morning with the sun kissing his forehead, announcing the arrival of the autumn. The garden, which was once so lovingly tended by Arvind's father, was in full bloom, resonating with the festivity that was around. The air was filled with the fragrance of divinity, as the flowers were getting restless in their impatience to adorn the goddess.

Aryan got up from the bed, and as a matter of habit, took the newspaper to the toilet. He looked at the mirror and while brushing his teeth, he remembered one of Kavya's cheesy remarks. Kavya used to tease Arvind and Aryan of their habit to carry the newspaper with them, when they went to the toilet for their morning ablution. She used to ask if they off-loaded the waste of the previous day or it was the crap called the news in the paper. The house had its own share of lighter moments that were hugely missing, since the spontaneity of events that unfurled after the unearthing of the chit fund fraud.

The bathroom was Aryan's comfort zone that allowed him to have his exclusive 'me-time' during a day. Two news items caught his attention, for he was connected with both in some way or the other. One of it screamed at him, announcing that Raghav and Priya were out of jail after furnishing bail. The other news at the right-hand bottom corner in the front page was about a scoundrel who had been imprisoned on the grounds of cheating in marriage. Rohan had made the headlines!

Aryan came out of the bathroom and noticed his mother occupied with her regular rituals in attending to the idols of the gods and goddesses. The woman had not failed a single day in bathing the stone idols in a concoction made of milk, honey and water, and then offering an elaborate feast of homemade sweets. The only exception were the days when women menstruate. The predominantly priestly practices and decrees consider women to be unclean to serve the gods during those days. The ease with which the women, mostly of his mother's age, had gladly embraced the diktats to be chastised as impure, made Aryan wonder oftentimes, if faith was a matter of fear or ignorance.

Aryan chose the convenience of being god-loving instead of god-fearing. He did not recollect airing his opinion on the subject, as it was an avoidable instance to be kept at bay. He was aware of the fact that present-day women were more evolved and were coming in droves to challenge the subjugation of women by the rotten patriarchal prejudices.

The mother and the son acknowledged each other over the morning tea. "Is there anything that you would want me to get from the market?" Aryan asked his mother.

"Kavya has already gone to the market and she will get the groceries and the vegetables. For the time being, why don't you get me the pouch of milk left by the milkman at the main gate and then get ready to go out to try your luck at the beauty salon," the mother replied sipping her tea, sounding as crisp as the toast of bread.

"It is a unisex styling and grooming salon and not just some neignbourhood hair cutting shop, Ma. Men and women visit these places with prior appointments, to end up spending in thousands to look better and feel greater," Aryan finished his breakfast and stomped off resentfully.

Aryan's walk took him past the place, which was once their home. So many people, unknown to him, inhabited it. He questioned his own brazenness, with which he had once challenged Raghav in their first encounter, when he had remarked that he would laugh the last and the loudest. It was almost impossible to get back a piece of dwelling in the high-rise with so many people already having made it their home. He sighed as he started walking the main street towards the market.

The most eminent club in the neighbourhood was seen to be getting ready for the Durga Puja. The members were seen putting up banners and festoons in their effort to publicize the magnificence of the approaching festivities. The hoardings were yelling at each other, flaunting the names of the celebrities, film stars, and politicians who would be gracing the occasion to inaugurate the annual extravaganza.

He came upon the eatery owned by Jeevan; that was extraordinarily bedecked in a riot of colors and suitably equipped in the contours of lip-smacking cuisines to extract the maximum moolah. People splurged on the food at his food joint during the annual gala affair. He stopped over for a cup of tea, not because he wanted to, but to look back at all those events associated with the place.

It was the place where he had met Arvind and his over enthusiastic credit card selling team. It was the place where he tried seeking a job and then failed miserably, asking for appointment from the prospective clients. He had seen Priya vanishing in Raghav's shining SUV. It was the place that offered him the brush with reality that he had the option to either remain a nincompoop for the rest of his life or announce his arrival by making a mark. The place was actually a pilgrimage; for he got the enlightenment on life and the surprises that were in store for him.

Aryan decided to go to Aesthetics and try out his luck with them. He was a trained stylist, but he did not have the experience with either the cuts or the curls to claim a job. He was thus, more or less convinced of the fact that it would be Priya's reference that might make the opportunity if any, to work in his favour. He was determined to make the move, there and then.

Aryan arrived at Aesthetics; it was 10.30 a.m. The salon had just opened as he noticed the staff entering the premises and moving towards the staff corner to change into their uniforms.

"Good morning sir, how may I help you?" a young man at the reception, enquired cheerfully.

"I am a trained stylist and I have come here looking for a job," Aryan replied without fumbling.

"You will have to go to the master franchise's office and enquire about the job opportunities. You must carry your bio-data and please be dressed for the occasion." The young man winked at him with a smile.

Aryan smiled back at him and thanked him while coming out of the salon. He cursed himself on having been irresponsibly hasty with presenting himself at the salon. Grooming and styling is all about self-presentation and it begins with the stylist! The young man at the reception was surely helpful.

"Hello, is this the Aesthetics office? I wish to speak to the Manager to seek an appointment for a job interview," Aryan enquired.

"Please note the email id and send in your bio-data. If you are found suitable, we will contact you after the festive season is over. There is a mad rush at all outlets and we are not conducting any job interviews these days." The voice of the woman on the other side of the phone sounded familiar.

"I will mail it and hopefully get to meet you when I come over for the interview," Aryan replied.

"You sound quite confident and I am sure you will get to work with us as we are opening some more outlets after the festivals. Aesthetics needs good people and I think you are one." The woman sounded quite reassuring and kind.

Aryan saw a glimmer of hope in the conversation that he had with her. He had to speak to Rhea to seek her help in creating an impressive bio-data. "Hello, Rhea?"

"What is it bhaiya? I am in the midst of something very important. Can this wait for some time?" Rhea sounded irritated.

"Rhea, I need your help in creating my bio-data. I have to email it at the earliest."

"Okay, relax bhaiya. I will send it to you by the end of the day today. But, please do not call me during the office hours. If it is urgent, leave me a message and I will get back to you at my convenience." Rhea disconnected the call without bothering to hear Aryan any further.

Aryan realized that Rhea did get to speak a lot amidst her busy schedule. He figured out what makes someone busy as he called out for his mother for some tea.

"Let me give you some company." That was Kavya.

"Kavya, do you know how to write a bio-data?" Aryan asked her innocently.

"Oh yes, I used to observe Arvind write his and I think I can surely help you write one for yourself." Kavya smiled as she settled down to help him.

"What will I do without you, Kavya?" Aryan looked at her in admiration and then bit his own tongue, realizing the inaptness of the otherwise harmless admission.

Kavya looked at him coyly. After creating the bio-data and helping Aryan chose a suitable email id, Kavya tenderly ran her fingers to ruffle his hair and went to the kitchen to help his mother.

It occurred to Aryan that it would not have been possible for Rhea to send him his bio-data in the absence of his email id and she did not even bother to ask if he had one! Although, he was hopeful that Rhea would call him at her convenience. The end of day did come, but Rhea's call did not; she was indeed busy as Aryan went to the cyber café.

The days went on as usual with Aryan's mother starting to frequent her 'symphony of sisters' at the temple, almost on a daily basis. He did not see much issue with it. Kavya used to frequent their place occasionally, but necessarily when Aryan's mother was at home. It did not require more than common sense for Aryan to comprehend, as to what would be holding back Kavya from coming downstairs in his mother's absence. He was in fact amused with the fickle-mindedness with their proposed food venture as the discussions between the two women in the house were more of a chance encounter with forced wordplay. The women did not need anyone but themselves, to cannibalize each other.

Aryan was gradually accepting and coming to terms with his own self. Rohan had taught him to outsmart the game of being an average while Rhea made him learn how to live the present by making the past irrelevant. In the meanwhile, Reema, who was in touch with Aryan, calling now and then to enquire about Aryan's mother and Rhea's career progress, started making herself not noticeable with the phone calls becoming a rarity.

Aryan's mother had made her displeasure quite clear with Aryan with his reciprocating to Reema. She still held Reema responsible for landing Rohan behind the bars. Aryan had tried reasoning out with his mother by sharing Reema's commitment to their relationship, but the elderly woman held onto her ground firmly. The woman was developing a strange and noticeable detachment with anything to do with either the house or its inhabitants. Aryan did not see any merit in stirring the hornet's nest any further.

However, whenever his mother was required to discuss Rohan with the women folk at the temple, she did not have any inhibition in proclaiming that Rohan was serving the prison term because of a lopsided legal provision. She conveniently erased the adultery episode. She overzealously protected Rohan against the tireless tirade made by the women in their interrogations and made them laugh at her back! Some of them were a special breed of literate fools who thrived on the spicy gossips. They were an insurmountable waste as humanity.

Aryan was counting his days as Durga Puja drew closer. His impatience was in anticipation to the email from Aesthetics, confirming the job interview. A visit to the cyber café in the evening became a regular feature. Thanks to the act of benevolence by his ex-employer, he could still carry some money in his wallet as he hardly spent anything on himself or on his modest lifestyle. He had nonetheless, started buying second hand lifestyle magazines which helped him to keep a tab of all the style in vogue, when it came to grooming and styling for men and women.

In was one of those regular evenings and Aryan was at home. He sat up noticing his mother enter the house from the temple. She asked him to stay back as she had to talk to him about something. The woman went to the washroom and emerged as pristine as the crisp white cotton starched sari that she was wearing. Aryan drew himself closer to her to be the sole audience.

"Aryan, my friends at the temple are planning to go on a pilgrimage after the Puja and I want to go along with them," she revealed her plans.

"That is fine with me, but who will take care of you all?" Aryan sounded supportive.

"The neighbourhood club is organising the pilgrimage and they are going to make all the necessary arrangements to attend to all the elderly people. I will need you to withdraw money from the bank, as the payment has to be made by the weekend. In the meanwhile, why don't you start looking for another place on rent? This house is too big for the two of us." Aryan's mother had made up her mind.

"Okay, I will do that." Aryan had barely gathered his wits after the sudden pronouncement when Kavya dropped in after a long time at their place.

"I hope I am not intruding. Actually, I need your advice on a matter. A pre-school chain had approached me to rent out the ground floor at an attractive price and I was wondering if I could go ahead with the proposal. The rooms are spacious enough and if both of you agree to move upstairs with me, it will serve the purpose," Kavya spoke uninterrupted, throwing a cold proposal at them.

"That won't be necessary Kavya. We were discussing something almost on the similar lines. Ma has asked me to look out for another place, as this place is too big for the two of us and we may end up saving some money on rent. Ma is leaving for a month-long pilgrimage after the Puja. Give me some time to find an alternate address while you go ahead with confirming the pre-school's offer," Aryan spoke to Kavya with a piercing look.

"I did not mean to ask you to vacate the place. I had come for your advice." Kavya had not been able to gather her conviction to extend the discussions any further.

"It is merely a coincidence that you chose to discuss your new tenants when we were planning to find a new address. So, there is no need to feel ill at ease." Aryan was defiant to Kavya's discomfort.

"What will happen to the food venture that we have been planning for some months now?" Kavya had directed the question at Aryan's mother who was feigning ignorance of the entire discussion that took place right in front of her.

"Let me come back from my pilgrimage," Aryan's mother replied icily, without taking her eyes off the television set.

"Fair enough, I think your pilgrimage is going to be a welcome break. I just hope I did not offend the two of you." Kavya gathered herself to leave the place.

"You must be kidding. There is nothing wrong with what you said. This is your house and you reserve the rights to offer tenancy to anyone at a better deal," Aryan's reply was evidently an invisible slap at Kavya's face.

The pilgrim had made progress with her hideous agenda, as she remained stoned to the television screen. Aryan was dumbfounded with himself with a sense of lingering despair in his heart. The emptiness within rebuked him of not having made any progress at all, when it came to understanding women.

The entire neighbourhood was resonating with the festive spirit around, with huge loud speakers earsplitting a vast range of Bollywood dance numbers, which was competing with the devotional songs with equal ease. No one cared about the music as long as the club members remained drunk and danced to the tunes of their patrons. The most illustrious of the patrons was Raghav. He was reincarnated as the messiah of the masses to have become a politician, upon his release from the jail on bail. Goddess Durga had descended on the earth with her troupe!

Aryan becomes the Prey

This is one time during the year, when every other thing comes to a standstill, but for celebrating the life in its fullest form and colours. Durga Puja in the city of Kolkata is the celebration of modernity fused with the tradition and culture. All the worries and grievances that people have with each other and their lives go for an annual sabbatical.

Bijoyadashami is the day that marks the end of the festivities, when the goddess goes back to *Kailash*. This is symbolized by the *Bisarjan* or the immersion of the deity in the holy Ganges, popularly known as the *Hoogly* in this part of the country. This is the day when the members from almost all the households, gather at the *pandal* to extend their warmth and love in bidding adieu to their proverbial daughter goddess Durga and her children.

Aryan's mother was not an exception to the annual ritual; something she had been practicing since time immemorial. The women at large, across all ages, wore the distinct red-bordered cotton *saris,* bedecked with trinkets and charms and the *sindoor* prominently declaring their marital status. The young and unmarried girls were not to be left behind in their ceremonial attire. The elderly and the widows exercised forced discretion in avoiding the bright and the red, in accordance to the unwritten societal dictate.

It is a feast for the eyes of any beholder to witness the spectacle, which starts with the *aarti* of the goddess, followed by the *sindoor khela* or the game of vermillion. The married women smear each other's face with the red vermillion, eventually breaking into a frenzied dance to the *dhaak* beats. Amidst the *ulu dhwani* and the blowing of the *shankho* or the conch shells, women offer sweets to one another, which denote the end of rituals, before the men folk take over for the bisarjan. The entourage of the local club takes the centre stage with their incredible snake dance to the cacophony of Bollywood chartbusters and the beats of the dhaak. One does not miss the moist eyes of the elderly people, upon realizing the inevitability of the closing stages of the festival with the immersion of the goddess.

The sky was lit bright in an orange hue. The sun that was about to set was found playing truant with the cotton clouds. The people, who did not want to be a part of the immersion procession, started dispersing to go back to the grind of their normal lives.

Aryan's mother exchanged pleasantries with those around her and her friends from the temple. She collected the prasaad as someone from within her group reminded her to confirm for the pilgrimage. She smiled at them, which was more of an endorsement. She retraced her steps back to her home, as Aryan was all alone. Kavya had requested for the prasaad or the devotional offering made to the goddess and shared by the devotees after the puja.

The evening was setting in with the sun down and the air had a nip in it. Aryan was clad in his casual wear with unkempt hair, carelessly caressing his strikingly handsome face with the sinewy muscles wanting to break free. His mother came back home while he was watching television. As she prepared to attend to the holy idols at home, she handed some flowers and sweets to Aryan and asked him to carry it upstairs for Kavya.

"I will wait for you over the tea, Aryan, once I am through with my evening prayers."

He gathered the flowers and the sweets and walked upstairs. The door was open, and the curtains tossed against the gentle breeze. The television was muted, but the radio set was playing a soulful instrumental. Kavya was lost in her thoughts, with her eyes fixed at the television, completely unaware that Aryan was in the room.

"*Shubho Bijoya*! Here are some sweets and prasaad for you," Aryan greeted Kavya as she leisurely rose up from her chair, switched off the television and her hands rose up to gather her hair in a bun. She looked incredibly beautiful in her red-bordered white sari, a dark red bindi on her forehead with a hint of the red vermillion in the parting of her hair. She took the sweets and the flowers from Aryan without reciprocating the greetings.

"What kept you back at home? You should have been at the rituals at the club," Aryan enquired as Kavya walked up to the door to shut it.

She appeared mysteriously menacing as she paced the room.

"I am married to someone who betrayed my trust. I wear the sindoor as it reminds me of my marital vows. I am in this attire not because of the occasion, but because I wanted to be. Now, I realize that this is not more than a representation of my servitude. I want to break free, to live a life on my own terms!"

Aryan suddenly felt like a castaway, marooned on an island as Kavya moved towards him. Everything around him looked so alien and hazy. He felt the savage run deep inside him as his body was fuming with the instinctive heat of a man, impatient to commit the original sin!

Kavya's kohl-lined dove like eyes and trembling lips were waiting in anticipation of a deep-throated reciprocation from him. She knew that her vulnerability was out of her own desire to submit herself to the inevitability of the impending act. She was poetry in motion as she explored every bit of Aryan, tearing off the clothes from his body. The wantonness of an aggrieved woman found the perfect suitor in a man, who was always hunting for a reassurance that he was never an average as a man. Aryan's self-discovery and Kavya's search for freedom culminated into the most unconditional and primitive compulsion of yielding to one another in an absolutely guilt-free act of making love.

Aryan won over his innate inhibitions in finding the ultimate bliss, when he lost himself between Kavya's heaving bosoms as she kept nurturing his exploits of her entire body. The adrenalin rush in Aryan made him entwine Kavya in a serpentine embrace, punctuating the breathlessness with a pause as he left his teeth marks all over her body.

The masculine rage of the warrior prince in the quest for every inch of Kavya, met with an equal match. Kavya did not show any signs of surrendering, without Aryan's pleading for mercy in getting more out of her. She marvelled at his insatiable energy with which he kept pounding her rhythmically, to the tunes of the instrumental music that was still playing on the radio. The window curtains voyeuristically rubbed against the walls in having witnessed the maiden act of ecstasy by the hermit in hiding!

Aryan lost his chastity belt as he lay beside Kavya and was coming to terms with the excruciating pain of the exhilarating delight. Kavya experienced a different kind of pain altogether. It was the pain of a relief as she had ended up invading the bastion of sanctity imposed upon by the obligations associated with marriage. All it took was an act of pleasure with her own body, but with someone she *chose*!

Aryan woke up from his state of stupor as he gathered his clothes and planted a gentle kiss on Kavya's forehead. He looked at his clothes in utter dismay as Kavya gave him a cold smile. Their eyes spoke to each other in regaling the moments of their togetherness. Kavya got up from the floor in her dishevelled looks that bore testimony to her struggle for breaking free and she dashed off to the bathroom.

"You stay back for some time Aryan, while I clean up. I will get you something to wear."

Aryan's eyes were at the door and he froze for a moment when he noticed that the door was partly open. The curtains were dancing to the gentle breeze. Kavya came out to the living room and handed him a fresh set of clothes. Aryan wanted to draw her attention to the doors, but held himself back. He put on Arvind's clothes and left her place with a question on his mind. Did someone witness them making love and tiptoed back?

On entering their house, Aryan found his mother arranging her clothes in a bag.

"I have been waiting for you to join me over tea, as it has been more than an hour that you left for that woman's place. Go and wash yourself thoroughly clean and get rid of Arvind's shirt. Put on something of your own!"

Aryan was stupefied at the speed with which the mystery behind the partially opened door got solved. He did not answer back his mother, but instead took the couch. As his mother poured over the tea to him, she spoke to herself completely regardful of his presence. "I have to make the payment for the pilgrimage tomorrow. Get me the money from the bank tomorrow."

One could hear the conch shells blowing vigorously amidst the shriek ululation. The dhakis started playing the pulsating beats, signalling the immersion procession or the journey of the goddess back to her heavenly abode. The goddess who was worshipped for five long days, morphed into clay, deep into the bed of the holy Ganges in signifying the cycle of life. The clay would be dug up the following year and the idol makers will turn into adept artisans in bequeathing divinity to the deity. Bijoyadashami is the day that symbolizes the triumph of good over evil, and hopefully, Kavya would want to mark it in her calendar as the day she stood liberated from the tyrannical social taboos.

The next day, at the break of dawn, Aryan woke up to find his tea by the bedside, and his mother unusually busy with herself in the kitchen. Without creating any ruckus, he finished his tea and went out for a walk. He did not have an iota of guilt him for what had transpired between the two consenting adults in the previous evening. But, he was definitely miffed with Kavya for not being careful with properly shutting the door.

The people, especially the school going children were trying hard to come to terms with the fact that the short vacation was over. He crossed the hotspot of the area, Jeevan's food joint, which was abuzz with the morning walkers relishing their tea, engrossed in their banter. Compared to the formative days, when Gitanjali was gearing to become what it had become these days, the morning walkers were ahead in their life style.

This remarkable transformation of the erstwhile sleepy neighbourhood of Gitanjali over the years had its share of a puny resilience. Aryan identified himself with it and those were the grocery stores, newspaper vendors, the government schools, the soccer, and cricket practicing at the neignbourhood clubs, the vegetable vendors, and the bidi smoking rickshaw pullers! The neighbourhood of Gitanjali had definitely moved up in its propensity to splurge, but for the soul and spirit of the locality. It still retained a typical middle-class majoritarian attitude in its opinions and views.

Aryan picked up his pace as he went back to his home. At the gate, he was greeted with a steely resolve from Kavya. "I have decided to rent out the ground floor by the end of this month as I am going to formalize the arrangement with the pre-school in a week from now. I will appreciate if you arrange to move out of this place at early as possible," she shot at Aryan and he was completely taken aback with her misdemeanour.

"That's not how you talk to someone who is not a stranger to you. If you are stressed with what happened yesterday, we must talk it out."

Aryan tried to bring some normalcy in their conversation, but to no avail.

"This is a new day and I am a new me. Plus, your mother still does not approve of your talking to a stranger." Kavya dashed off to the street as Aryan stood in absolute bewilderment.

Kavya was indeed a strong woman, he thought to himself as he walked inside his home.

"I have never seen or heard of a fire without a smoke," his mother remarked as she served breakfast.

There have been numerous occasions in Aryan's life when he felt choked with insult, but he had never taken the offence on his food. He finished eating and got ready to leave the house. He had a simpler checklist with him this time. First, he would check his email account for the job interview at Aesthetics and then he would go to the bank to withdraw money for his mother, and finally start looking a place on rent. "Ma, I am leaving and we must get ready to move to a new place on rent. We have been served a notice by the landlady."

His mother remained unmoved while attending to the household chores. She was losing one battle after the other and starting to lose the sight of the war!

Aryan checked the email inbox and much to his anticipation, the appointment for the job interview was there for him to note down some essential details. He walked out of the cyber café with a renewed sense of self-assurance. He wished for two things at that very moment. He wished that his father was alive, and that he had a bike with him when he figured a pretty girl walking down the street. He was no less than a hero to himself. But only if he had a bike! He thought of calling up Rhea, but then decided against it, as he had merely landed himself with an interview and not the job. Moreover, Rhea would be too busy at that hour in the day. Then he thought of Priya. She would have been glad to know that Aryan was about to make a career of his choice.

The interview was scheduled in a week's time, and thus, Aryan decided to make good use of the time by looking for a place on rent. Kavya had become conspicuous by her absence at their place, which fuelled his mother's frequent and sharper abuse for her, especially in Aryan's presence. In the rarest of occasions when they crossed each other's path, Kavya was courteous to acknowledge him, but did not forget to remind him of the urgency to vacate the place. On one such occasion, Aryan chose to confront her.

"Why are you doing this to me? What makes you think that I will be ridden with the guilt of having trespassed upon the honour of our relationship? I think, whatever happened between the two of us was consensual and spontaneous. I do not see any sense in this uneasiness of your silent rebuke whenever we come face to face."

Kavya held her breadth for a moment and spoke with astonishing firmness, "Aryan, the encounter was consensual, but it was by design. I do not wish to judge you, but I know one thing for sure. I wanted to hurt Arvind. Two people found the door partially open on that fateful day. One was you and the other person was *Arvind*! I had received a letter from him, informing me that he would be coming to meet me in the evening of Bijoyadashami. He wanted to discuss reconciliation measures. You got a heart? Get hurt to get going!"

As Kavya left him in the lurch, Aryan found himself caught in a whirlpool of deceit and unbridled desire. The admission by Kavya made it amply clear to him that she did not have any interest in him and wanted him to be man enough to take the event in his stride. Aryan realized that she was grievously hurt on having been spurned.

Arvind had preferred not to confide to her of his dubious deals, which made Kavya become irresistibly irreverent to their marital vows. She did not care to be judged by anyone as her love for Arvind remained uncompromising, but conditional on the grounds of mutual respect and trust. Aryan hoped that Kavya did not remain hurt forever, for she had punished Arvind in her own way for his betrayal. It was a different thing altogether that she chose an easy prey in him!

Aryan's relationship with his mother had become very formal and got restricted to brief exchange of words. He mostly kept to himself, turning pages of the second hand magazines to browse through the styling and grooming statements in the fashion industry. He had also developed a liking for taking early morning walks in the neighbourhood. It gave him the much-needed respite from the suffocating relationship that had unfortunately grown between him and his mother. In one of those early morning walks, he chanced upon a '*to let*' sign in one of the houses, and he took down the contact details. The only thing that remained his immediate priority was to land himself with the job as a stylist with Aesthetics.

The day came when Aryan was to appear for his interview. He kept his mother posted of the date and was in for a pleasant surprise to find his trousers and a formal shirt by his bedside, neatly pressed for the occasion. He immediately recognised the shirt that his father used to wear for his monthly performance review meetings to his office. A starched and neatly folded handkerchief was placed alongside the dress, with some crisp currency notes. Aryan got dressed for the occasion and found his mother at the door.

Aryan bowed down to touch her feet. "Aryan, I will be leaving for my pilgrimage in two days from now. Get me some real good news today, before I leave for my atonement and peace."

"Ma, I will get you the news that you want to hear. I will be meeting the new landlord on my way back and we will have a new place for ourselves."

"I wish, Rohan, Reema and Rhea were around today!" His mother wiped her tears as she spoke.

"One at a time, Ma. First, let me come back with the confirmation of the job and then you will find that every other thing will gradually fall in place, all by themselves. And, thank you for the shirt and the handkerchief." Aryan's mother smiled at him as he left home to conquer the world.

The lifestyle industry in the country had undergone a complete transformation with the presence of international products and services. The young generations worship their style icons more than god. The consistent increase in the number of super rich and very wealthy high networth individuals and families had augmented the lifestyle industry with their lavish spending on cosmetics, beauty, wellness, styling and grooming. Anybody who has the money wants to look and feel good about themselves.

Aesthetics dominated the national landscape of the organised segment in beauty, wellness and hairstyling products and services. It had earned an enviable repute in a very short span of time for itself as a branded salon.

The ambience, hygiene, quality of products and services not only attracted the affluent class, but created an aspiration in the budget class as well, who did not mind swiping their credit cards to be counted as clients. It had become a styling destination for the fashion conscious and counted many celebrities, socialites, elite industrialists, and politicians as their clients. The biggest contribution, however, was its influence in shaping the career option for many a people like Aryan, who found it a relief. They had no urge to participate in the rat race. The society was accepting the fact that first impressions for people were indeed created by the stylists, for lasting impressions. And, it did matter!

Aryan was at the corporate office of Aesthetics, well in time. He noticed the exchange of cautious glances among some other candidates, who had come for the interview. He handed over the call letter for the interview to the woman at the front office and did not forget to thank Kavya in his mind, for having helped him in creating the same. The interview seemed more of a formality to Aryan as he sailed through the process without any hiccups. He was offered the role of a junior stylist with the most prestigious address of Aesthetics chain. He could not complain on the remuneration that came along with it.

Aryan was super excited and it was palpable. He had finally made it to his dream career! He made no efforts to hide it when he went to thank the woman at the front desk.

She smiled at him and acknowledged his enthusiasm while explaining to him the joining formalities. She looked familiar to him in the first instance, but he did not to waste any time by enquiring. He was getting restless to breathe some fresh air, out in the open and talk to his mother and Rhea.

Sanity prevailed upon him when he came out in the streets. He called up the prospective property owner, fixed up the time to meet him. The events were unfolding as if the pages of a book were turning, bookmarked to occur one after the other. He met up with the owner and completed the documentation to work out the plans in relocating by the end of the month. Then, he called up Rhea and was glad that she answered his call.

"Rhea, I have got the job with Aesthetics and will be joining them from next month."

"I am glad you called, as I was about to call you. I will be in Kolkata very soon to start working on the RGV Enterprises scam again."

"But, is the issue still alive? I learnt from the newspapers that the investigation files are gathering dust while the judicial inquiry is on, but none of the people have got back their money."

"Most of what you get to read in the newspaper or get to know by watching the television is politically motivated. The media is an active pawn in the political ploys. Just wait, until I come down and re-open the probe. And yes, Raghav has switched over his loyalty and has new masters to take orders from."

"When are you coming home? We are about to shift to a new place by this month end and Ma is leaving for her pilgrimage tomorrow."

"Bhaiya, I am coming over on an official assignment and I will be staying in a hotel and not your place. You do not have to mention my visit to Ma. Let her leave in peace for her pilgrimage."

"Rhea, I have got a job as a stylist at the Aesthetics." Aryan realized that Rhea had disconnected her phone.

Aryan's visit to the Howrah station with his mother was after ages and it invoked some fond memories of their only vacation as a family, many years back, to Puri in Odisha. His mother was extremely composed as against the commotion and cacophony, which was being made by the visibly excited travellers who were to begin their pilgrimage. Aryan bought some dry foods, fruits, and water for his mother.

"The tour operator would be taking care of all these things." She accepted all of it willingly and kept in her bag.

"Never mind Ma, keep these with you, and share it with your friends from the temple. You have a mobile phone with you; keep me posted of your travel and experiences."

"Do not worry about me. I am feeling bad that I am leaving you all alone, in so many years. Be careful with shifting the household items and belongings and hire some people to help with it."

"Stop pampering me Ma, I am a grown-up man. I will arrange everything in order and start going to my new job from our new house."

"Take care of Rhea and Rohan when I am not around."

Aryan lost no more time in helping her mother settle with her bags and belongings with her reserved seat in the train compartment. He exchanged the contact coordinates with the tour operator as he bid her goodbye. As he took the bus back to their house, he tried to figure out his mother's words while she was leaving. Rohan and Rhea had long outgrown him to take care of themselves and their lives.

Once he came back home, Aryan found it a little unusual to be alone. It seemed to be a luxury uncalled for, to be in the place with nothing to share with anyone! He had read about that exceptional state of being, that a few could indulge. It came at the cost of solitude. It was as if he was in a treasure hunt, while rummaging through the things in the house.

The house was always big enough for all of them, for they had never planned to stay apart from one another. The family had sparse furniture and fixtures that were made over a long period of time, when his parents had just started their family. Most of the kitchen appliances were old enough to be sold as trash, but for the two trusted lieutenants in the refrigerator and the mixer-grinding machine, which withstood the test of time to primarily serve his mother in all her battles.

It was becoming difficult for him to stay still, unsure of what to do next and thus he chose to go for an early dinner. He had bananas, cold milk and bread, without even bothering to check the refrigerator if it held any solace for him in store. He had become a loner in his mother's absence!

After dinner, he started organising the wardrobe in the cabinet that he used to share with his brother, until he left home for his studies. The only other cupboard in the house belonged to his mother, which she shared with Rhea. His father was immodestly organised with his documents and personal belonging. He had two big worn-out suitcases, which served throughout his lifetime. In the absence of his mother, the house seemed to have lost its harmony with holiness, when he realized not having lit the incense sticks in the evening after he returned home from the station.

Aryan realized that it would be an arduous task for him to attend to the packaging of the entire household items and thus decided to engage some porters for the job. His mother had left him with some lump sum amount of money towards the relocation and the payment for advance to the new landlord. He thus chose to attend to the stately affair of relocating as per his mother's advice and crashed into the sofa to catch some sleep. It was impossible to fall asleep knowing very well that his mother would not be around to wake him up in the morning with the tea by the bedside. The woman was omnipresent in her absence and that made Aryan feel guilty for a moment. He had taken his mother for granted and now that she was not around, it was difficult to accept it.

As his mind kept wondering about the strength of the umbilical cord, it wandered about the present-day whereabouts of his siblings. It would be two years very soon, when Rohan would be coming out of his imprisonment. Although he remembered the date of his release, he never had the urge to visit him at prison. His mother did not insist even once to prevail over Aryan's indifference towards Rohan, while he was behind the bars. How would Rohan reach out to him after he was released from jail? Aryan thought of leaving behind the address of the new house with Kavya. What about Reema? They had not spoken to each other since the day she had last come to see them at their place.

Aryan felt a little sad for having let his pre-occupation with himself make him out of reach from his own people. Rhea's transformation from a docile girl into a passionate career crusader was one of his biggest astonishments. He thought that her professionalism was getting overshadowed by the indifference towards her family and was gradually getting bordered around self-centeredness. Ever since she earned herself a decent name in the media and the political circle through the unearthing of the RGV Enterprises scam, she had been singularly furthering her only cause to be in the eternal limelight. It did hurt Aryan that she did not even spare a thought to congratulate him on landing a job and despite her knowing, she did not even call once to speak to their mother, before she left for her pilgrimage!

Aryan was getting mired in his thoughts when he received the phone call from his mother. Battling heavy eyelids, he heard his mother with a childlike glee, "Aryan, have you had your dinner? I forgot to mention that I have cooked some meals that will last you for a couple of days. It is in the refrigerator; please warm up the food a little before having it." He went off to his sleep, peacefully!

Aryan woke up at his usual time in the morning, but did not feel adventurous to get into the kitchen to make himself tea. He promised himself to start his experiment in the kitchen from the next day and have his tea and breakfast at one of the more familiar early morning food joints that he was comfortable with to be his normal self. He, however, regretted the fact that his relationship with Kavya had reached such predictable ebb, that there was no way either of them would want to rekindle the familiar vibes for the sake of a cup of tea! He laughed out loud all by himself, at the weird possibility before leaving the house.

At the breakfast joint, the crowd of people came across as accessible and modest with their life and times. He overheard the discussions centered on some people lending their advices to some others, seeking compassion on issues with work and at home. The relatively younger men were discussing the trauma associated with finding the right tutor for their children. Most of them had common grounds of discussion, which included the skyrocketing prices of essential commodities, lowering of interest rates in the bank and lastly the dichotomy of the federal relationship between the central and the state government in our country.

A new government was in power at the center, backed with an overwhelming majority. It ensured consistent northbound bourses for the capitalists and the investors and kept parroting the agenda for all-round development, uprooting corruption and generating employment opportunities. Many people felt that the government's policies and promises were high on intent, mediocre on content, but proved dismal in its delivery.

Some others were unwavering to admit the lapses. They were of the view that the overhauling of the corrupt system post-independence required people to be patient. They cited the statistical figures of benevolence by the central government and took immense pride in getting globally acknowledged as the nation in waiting to be counted among the top of economic powers. They condemned the previous government of indecisiveness and showered praise on the current government for their 'truth-be-told-at-the-face' attitude.

Countless opinions and still counting as Aryan realized the influence of the fourth estate as one of the four pillars of democracy. The middle class, which was the dutiful tax payers and consisted of the majority of the voters, found solace in getting a direction to their problems by reading the newspapers and watching the news. What the people ignored was the possibility that the directions to the issues confronting the common people actually got drafted by the political parties. It was designed by the divisive politics of caste and religion and immaculately delivered by the prime-time news and the morning headlines in the newspaper.

Opinions were getting monetized by the media at every opportunity available, to keep the voters engrossed with the reluctance to accept facts over fiction. The well-oiled machinery kept on working overtime in widening the ever-growing rift between people. The differences in opinion were getting pampered and patronized in the excuse of democracy for our country, which has historically been ruled and seldom governed.

Aryan's first day in the new house was spent unpacking the goods and storing them randomly across the entire living room and the kitchen. The house had a living room with a dining space, two bedrooms, and a kitchen. The fresh coat of cheap distemper paint was strong and nauseating, but Aryan did not have a choice but to start acclimatizing himself with the place that had become their home. He somehow managed to make enough room for himself in one of the bedrooms and unpacked his wardrobe. He left the rest of the household items unattended, until his mother returned from her pilgrimage.

While leaving the previous house, he had handed over the keys to the ground floor to Kavya and left behind their new address, requesting her to share it with Rohan if he ever returned looking for them. Aryan did not take cognizance of Kavya remaining unmoved and maintaining an unfriendly silence, for all that he treasured were his memories with the house. It was the house where they took shelter when Raghav had rendered them homeless, after his father's death.

Five years of their stay saw the extraordinary transformation of Rhea into a confident and successful modern woman. The family also went through the pain of Rohan and Reema's separation. It was the place where he had learnt what it took to become a man from Arvind and then started his career at the store. He came to know Kavya primarily as a friend on whom he could fall back upon, and then as a woman, to eventually become the prey in her game of vengeance. The house would always remain an unavoidable anchor in his life.

Aryan had ten days to start his career afresh with Aesthetics. He spent most of his time in flipping through the various magazines on fashion, food and travel, and enjoyed reading about new places, experiences and the constantly changing lifestyle of the rich and famous. He continued with his leisurely walks in the mornings and the mandatory stop at the food joint that he had started counting as one of his favourite places to relax and be with himself.

Much to his surprise, he was picking up his skill with preparing basic meals and found peace in attending to the deities at home in the evenings. In fact, he had started unpacking the other household items and organised them at various places in the house, hoping that his mother would be glad to find her house in order when she came back from her pilgrimage.

In one of those afternoons during his forced sabbatical while Aryan was relaxing, he received a call from Rhea asking him to meet her up at the hotel, late in the evening. She was in the city for her assignment with the television channel. Aryan noticed quite a number of calls from an unknown phone, which he had missed during his conversation with Rhea and he returned the call. The person on the other side, who was frantically trying to reach him, was the tour operator who sounded livid out of his helplessness. Aryan's mother had been missing at Varanasi for almost two days. The tour operator had filed a report at the police station and Aryan's details were furnished as the next of kin, which would require him to travel to Varanasi and get in touch with the police for details.

Aryan called up Rhea to inform her of the development, which would require them to travel to Varanasi.

"What is it with you bhaiya? We are to meet a little later in the evening and I am in a very important meeting."

"Rhea, there is something more crucial than your important meetings. Ma is missing! I am on my way to your hotel. You get ready to leave for the station as we have to take the earliest available train."

Rhea was startled at first with Aryan's assertion. Aryan was no longer the ordinary man, as she felt secured and confident to comply with his directive. Circumstances had forced Rhea to become bold and possibly aggressive with the world around her, but then, she felt at ease with her elder brother taking control of the situation. She packed her bags, called up her office and waited in her room to accompany Aryan to Varanasi.

While in the train, Rhea thought to herself that the trip to Varanasi had two objectives. It was about bonding beyond the realms of a relationship as a brother and a sister and find out their mother. The idea was to discover what was missing and possibly start working towards reinforcing the missing links. They reached Varanasi the following morning, thanks to Rhea's professional network, which got them the reservations in the train.

Their hotel was at a location quaintly named as *Englishiya Line*, close to the cantonment and the railway junction. The hotel was a decent one and was fairly living up to its reputation with the buffet spread for the breakfast, crisp morning newspaper, travel desk, prompt room service, laundry service, and a fantastic line of cooks for the north Indian cuisine. The only avoidable sight was that of a huge durbaan with his mustachioed *salaams* every now and then, curtly reminding of the *bakshish* that he was entitled to, at the time of the checkout!

After having their breakfast, they went to the police station to seek first hand status check of their mother. The officer in charge was cordial, considering the fact that the orders that must have been already barked off to him from relevantly higher officials. He assured them with all the assistance in finding out their mother. The day was never supposed to be a relaxed one as they ended up planning a detailed city tour, not wanting to miss anything and everything that the city had to offer and keep scouting for places of interest by the pilgrims, in the hope of finding their mother.

They went to the Kashi Vishwanath temple, one of the most revered *jyotirlingas*. The vulture-like eyes of the religious escorts or the pundits, as they want to be addressed to, caught them off guard. They had to accost a couple, but successfully reasoned out with a blatant lie, that they were familiar with the temple terrain. One of the more adventurous pundits came within a menacing proximity to establish his rights to guide them to the temple. Aryan's reaction was a spur of the moment defensive act to whisk him off by confronting him in chaste Hindi. Which if translated, would imply, "take a fly, I am a badass!" Rhea felt reassured with what Aryan did, as he clasped her hands in comforting her.

The rituals at the temple included the invite by the shopkeepers to lodge one's cell phone, shoes, leather accessories, and camera in the lockers. The actual idea was to sell the offerings (prasaad) for the presiding deity and his consort.

The gimmick of monetizing the fear for god yielded a handsome return for all the middlemen. They had become the coercive medium for many of the hapless devotees in their atonement for countless sins, which they may not have even committed. The only hope for the devotees in return of the offerings made to the gods remained with a belief of freeing oneself from the cycle of re-birth, or to attain nirvana. After performing the rituals, they gave a miss to an iconic landmark, called the 'Kachouri galli' for the want of time as they moved towards the ghats.

The boat ride was something that Rhea wanted to avoid, but for the insisting eyes of Aryan which implored for and wanted a *yes* from her. Looking at the receding water levels, Aryan let the brave man in him scout for a boatman. There was a bevy of them as he singled out Manoj from the crowd. He was in for a pleasant surprise when he offered him the one-hour cruise on the Ganges at a discount. Aryan caught the silent approval in Rhea's eyes.

The one-hour cruise on the Ganga was near normal as an experience that they had expected it to be. They spent the time less in admiring the ghats and the chequered history behind them, but more with discussing Manoj and his life and the times.

Varanasi is known as a city of temples, a sobriquet that comes from the vastness of appeal when it comes to faith. The Gyanvapi mosque, the St. Thomas Church, the Buddhist pagodas and the Jain temples add to its religious flavour. It is a pilgrimage for the god-fearing masses learning to accept and convert into god-loving souls. A beautiful example to promote the grandeur of unity in diversity is further exhibited in the resplendence of the *sandhya aarti* at the Ghats in the evening. It witnesses a gathering of people from different religious faiths as they get immersed in the spell of the Vedic chants, amidst the serenity of the flowing Ganges. Varanasi is a city to renounce the abject miseries associated with rituals and learn the virtues of belief!

The next day, Aryan and Rhea were to travel to Sarnath and Rampur fort.

Driving in the city of Varanasi required no less than acrobatic skill. Aryan had heard of the bulls blocking the movement, but then the fancy electric carriages were the new-age bulls. Rhea drew Aryan's attention to an alley that had converted to a road with concrete dividers paving the one-way rule. SUVs, MUVs, hatchbacks, sedans, rickshaws, autos, two-wheelers and the e-autos plying were vying for their share of the pie on the roads! Their driver Kamlesh had a word of wisdom to offer, "If you are a Bhaiyaji, a Bahubali or the ruling party's sycophant flaunting the party's flag in your Scorpio, you will be counted as the first among equals!"

The drive took them across the heart of the city as both of them were making silent notes with preying eyes for their mother. They kept riding the car across the dugout roads, imposing concrete layouts for the flyovers, the momo shops, the biriyani joints, the on-shop thanda beer outlets and the shopping malls with dozens of tolerant mannequins braving the heat and dust.

After a near comfortable ride to the Sarnath ruins and the museum, admiring the ASI's (Archaeological Survey of India) work on excavation and restoration over the years, they drove to the Rampur fort. They had lip-smacking chaats and lassi as their lunch for the day and then drove to back to the city of Varanasi.

Aryan actually found a new reason to take Rhea seriously. People around were addressing her as 'Madamji' and she found it very convenient to wield the newfound authority. Be it with crossing the roads or when she was being offered additional privileges, either at the temple or at the ghats! The feeling was short-lived as Aryan discovered that it was Rhea's near perfect Hindi diction to be the real reason behind the new-found fame! Staying at New Delhi had done some real confidence building for her.

In the morning of the third day of their stay in Varanasi, Rhea confided in Aryan that she was finding no sense in wasting any further time to look out for their mother in Varanasi. They had two choices in front of them. The first one was to either depend upon the police to do their job or keep on with their search, which had been in vain during the last two days. Aryan found merit with what Rhea suggested as he had to join Aesthetics in a few days and Rhea had her assignments.

Aryan was also consciously embarrassed of the fact that her younger sister was footing all the travel bills and the cost of the food and the two rooms in the hotel. He was, however, a little doubtful if the police would put in efforts. He was finding it strange that the mobile phone, which his mother was carrying with her, was not helping the police to trace her location!

"So, what did you decide bhaiya?"

"I think you make sense with what you said. Let us leave the police to do their job while you leverage your professional network as a journalist to get faster results."

"So, do I arrange for our travelling back?"

"Yes, let's get back to Kolkata and pray that Ma is safe wherever she is."

"I will have to get back to New Delhi and come back for my investigations later."

"Now, that's disappointing. Just when we started cherishing our days together after a long time, you want to go back to New Delhi?"

"Bhaiya, that's where I belong and I have a job to keep," she smiled affectionately at Aryan.

Aesthetics

Aesthetics at the Central Park in Kolkata distinctively stood out as one of the most prominent landmarks in the vicinity. It was the anchor and master outlet of the salon in the city and was known to be the latest hunting ground for the who's who, when it came to their styling, grooming, and wellness. The chain of salons from Aesthetics had set its footprints some five years back in the city as a part of its national presence and it had taken very little time for the anchor outlet to pave the path for many more branches across the entire city.

The swanky 3000 square feet of the beauty and wellness extended unparallel courtesies. The men got the cologne-dipped hand towels while the women received lavender-soaked face towels the moment they stepped inside the salon. The plush sofas and the recliners in the customer's lounge made the customers in waiting feel comfortable over either the iced-tea or the green tea for the discerning ones. The entire area was climatically conditioned and the in-house cafeteria remained busy with selling health drinks, aromatic oils, and organic health supplements. The ambience was engineered with soothing lights and artefacts that made the first timers marvel at the brains behind the business!

The colour of the uniforms helped in identifying the stylists and therapists from the assistants. The muted colours of different hues served as an easy guide to locate the styling areas from the wellness zone and the spa. Many of the regular clients found it convenient to transact and conclude their businesses and celebrate their deals over the fresh juices and salads. Aesthetics was clearly redefining the power corridors in conducting business as the discussions at the golf course were gradually finding it easy to move to the iconic address at the Central Park.

The imposing front elevation, right on the high street attracted the clientele, but the real secret behind retaining the loyalty were the first in class stylists, beauticians and therapists with Aesthetics. There were some exceptional instances when some of the top-notch clients went a step further, by sharing their Google calendar with their preferred service providers and ensured a steady flow of newer clients through their word of mouth referrals.

Bipasha was one such resource, who was carefully crafted by the almighty with the right proportion of beauty and brains. She was endearing with her conversations with the regular clients, but also careful with the wannabes who wished to be included in her coveted inner circle. One of them was Karan Seth, a portly gentleman with receding hairlines, well in his fifties. Bipasha considered it an arrangement in mutual convenience to spend her time beyond the working hours with various men. She had been out with Karan on more than one occasion. She was a woman in her early forties and had gone through a divorce from an abusive husband.

She was very particular with choosing her company of acquaintances, as she was sure that most of the men were simply attracted to her physically and every one of them wanted to get her laid. It never occurred to that lascivious lot that she had her own ambitions and was actually looking for an investor among them, to start her own business in beauty and wellness. Karan Seth was an exception, and thus, he enjoyed her company more often, to the visible cravings from other hopefuls.

At work, she had carved a niche for herself with her constant yearning for learning in expanding her domain knowledge and its applications. She was well ensconced in her position as one of the senior-most beauticians, but never allowed the crown to consign her ambitions to the back seat. She had her focus and plans in place to become the closest competitor to Aesthetics!

If anyone who had the matching skills and the temperament to pose a threat to Bipasha, it was Nagma. A gutsy young woman strikingly attractive, she had a guaranteed audience to her opinions on almost any topic under the sun! She was extremely committed to her family, which consisted of her father who was ailing with pulmonary disorder and a bright young bother, pursuing his studies in medicine. Having lost her mother while undergoing her post-graduation, she had to give up her dreams to become a research scholar when she took up the responsibility to take care of her father and support her brother's education.

It was possibly the critical conversations, due to her academic background, that made her popular with her colleagues and her clients alike, especially, with the non-conformists. Nagma was pre-occupied with her family. It rarely came to her mind that she was a contender to the crown of being the principal beautician, which made Bipasha avoid any bickering with her at the work place. Nagma's biggest hope was with her brother graduating as a doctor. She yearned to go to some of the exotic places on vacation that she had heard about from her clients. Her preferred breather was to hang around with Roselyn at the neighbourhood, tasting spicy savories over tea.

Roselyn hailed from the picturesque north-eastern states of India and was quite often mistaken as someone from the distant Thailand. She had migrated from Shillong in Meghalaya, where her father was a shopkeeper and attended to their farms that produced pineapples and potatoes. Roselyn was enigmatically pristine, as unspoiled as her faraway home in the mountains. She had one of her colleagues called Kanwal, smitten by her cuteness, which was overloaded with innocence, especially when she sang unmindfully in her lilting soft voice.

Kanwal belonged to a wealthy business family who attached a lot of importance to family values, fiery food, and frivolous fun. The awesome food that came along with

Kanwal every day had found a devoted fan in Roselyn, whose cheeks would turn red with every bite of the food, but she would keep asking for more and more. Kanwal took extra attention and care for the demure girl as Roselyn found him to be the knight in a shining armour.

Kanwal was a diligent learner and his idol was Rehan, who was the principal stylist. He worked closely with Rana who was waiting in the wings to be the next big sensation in styling and grooming. The crown of being the most sought-after stylist came with a lot of thorns, but Rehan wore it with élan and ease. He had loads of attitude and no one ever dared to cross the line with Rehan, as he was the blue-eyed boy at the salon.

Rehan was known to blow away most of his earnings on his wild ways and took pride in admitting to being a serial womanizer. While at work, Rehan kept to himself and enjoyed every bit of his fame, occasionally transgressing the professional limits with the clients. Kanwal had noticed that Rana and Rehan were fierce competitors at the workplace, which brought out the best in them. When it came to finding a respite from the demanding schedule, it was very heartening to note that they buried their hatchet in holding and lighting a cigarette for one another and breaking into laughter, sharing their exploits beyond work!

The prankster of the lot was Samir, who was notorious for creating all kinds of confusion and ending up offending someone or the other at the workplace. He was reprimanded very often for cracking silly jokes at the expense of some odd clients. Samir was gifted with comic timings and mimicry. He took a lot of pride in being Rehan's sidekick, running errands for him, and massaging his bloated ego as a seasoned sycophant. Very little was known about his antecedents but for the fact that he had towed along with Rehan when he had joined Aesthetics.

The staff canteen was the favourite hangout zone for the staff, which was, however, very cleverly designed to dissuade the employees from getting into unnecessary babble. It could accommodate people in batches of not more than five or six at a time. It was the only place in the salon during the regimented lunch break for an hour, when the people could take off their masks to be their normal selves. At times, the canteen converted into classrooms when some trainers would drop in to discuss the latest fads and conduct hands-on practical sessions in cuts and curls.

Aesthetics was synonymous with the bold and the beautiful and the credit was rightly extended to a dynamic lady, Ms Priya Kaul, who was responsible for steering the business to a profitable venture, much ahead of the plans and to the delight of the promoters.

The dream comes true

There had been no news from the Varanasi police. Rhea was initially in touch with Aryan after their return from Varanasi. The phone calls, gradually, became infrequent. Aryan made no issue about it when they spoke to each other as he was gradually accepting the fact that she was working hard to make a mark for herself in the extremely competitive space of investigative journalism at a national level. His heart ached for his mother, particularly in the evenings, when he attended to the evening prayer at home.

The new landlord was indifferent after making some initial enquiry about his mother. His inquisitiveness died down as the whole neighbourhood was aware of his mother having gone missing from Varanasi. The pilgrims were back and that explained the progress of the news, travelling so fast from the temple corridors to every nook and corner of Gitanjali.

It was the first working day of the month and Aryan was back to their new house, after his morning stroll. The day was significant as he was about to begin the second innings of his career as a stylist. He was ready to leave the house for the first day at Aesthetics as he overcame the raw emotions in leaving behind an empty house for the first time in his life.

It was 9.00 a.m., when Aryan started ascending the stairs of the grand salon. At the reception, he was in for a pleasant surprise, to be ushered in with many warm smiles. He instantly remembered the lady at the front desk from the day of his interview at Aesthetics. It was actually the same woman who had helped him with the address and contact number of Priya, when he went to the styling and grooming school in search of her. The familiarity with a person whom he had met briefly calmed his nerves as he settled down at the men's room. He was changing his clothes to put on the uniform when Samir entered the room and started reciting an old nursery rhyme, "Chubby cheeks, dimple chin, rosy lips, teeth within, curly hair, very fair, eyes are blue, lovely too. Madam's pet, is that you? Would you know this from your school days?" Samir asked.

"No, I did not go to an English medium school," replied Aryan.

"That actually makes sense as you are a handsome man, but without the rosy lips or the blue eyes. Anyway, I am Samir."

"Thank you. But what did you mean by Madam's pet?"

"Oh! Forget it. It is a silly nursery rhyme. I am Rehan's assistant and he is the god over here."

"Good to know, and I am Aryan, and I have joined here as a stylist."

"Not yet my friend, wait till you get tagged onto a senior to learn the tricks of the trade. You become a stylist only when Madam approves of it."

"So, who do I get to work with to begin with and who is our Madam?"

"You will get to know her very soon. Angela will tell you with whom do you start your training. I will see you at the lunch break." Samir left him with a mischievous wink as Aryan gave the last minutes touches before stepping out of the washroom.

"Aryan, I am Angela and I look after the administration, but do not ask me what are the others things that I do in my role. It is almost anything and everything to do with you all and the clients as well." Angela was brimming with self-pride as she spoke.

"Do you remember me?" asked Aryan.

"Yes I do, and you are here because Priya madam wanted it that way."

That explained the cakewalk at the interview for Aryan. He always wondered why he was not asked to give any demonstration of his work after the interview. Now that he knew it was Ms Priya Kaul's recommendation which got him the job; he had to prove himself in the craft of styling and grooming. He had to let his work speak for itself, instead of being madam's pet!

Angela introduced him to Bipasha, "Bipasha is going to be your mentor to begin with, and once she finds you ready with the beauty treatments, she will recommend you to work with Rehan."

"Hello Aryan, I am Bipasha."

Aryan remembered Kavya's advice not to stare at women as he gathered his admiration for Bipasha and returned a smile. Observing Bipasha attending to the clients with her feline movements and the deftness of her fingers was a pleasure. It was a treat for any newcomer like Aryan to watch one of the master artists, effortlessly transforming the plain woman to become attractive and a confident lady. The sophistication with which she conducted her business made her endearingly assertive, whom the clients could hardly refuse. Although it was difficult to attend to all the clients simultaneously, she made Aryan attend to the clients in the lobby to ensure that they did not miss the complimentary beverages while browsing the reading materials.

Aryan was cheerfully attending to the clients and helping Bipasha with arranging the various tools for her craft at the styling station. During the course of the stimulating conversation that Bipasha was having with the clients, Aryan picked up the art of promoting various extended services available with the salon. It ranged from skin health, facial, foot care, nail manicures, aromatherapy, oxygen therapy, mud bath, and even meditation!

Clients who had originally come in for a regular hair care or facial were lured for waxing and threading along with the sun tan treatment. Bipasha was skillfully making them believe that an enhanced self-esteem came by the way one carried themselves. They were falling for the bait. It was all about looking great, feeling good, and winning ways through the world!

"Aryan, would you be comfortable with attending to Anamika for her manicure?" The request from Bipasha sounded more of an instruction as he nodded to arrange the cart and the trolley.

"Who is this young man?" asked Anamika.

"He is Aryan and he has joined today. He is currently going through warm up and a familiarization with Aesthetics before wielding the knives and the scissors himself," Bipasha spoke encouragingly about Aryan and that surely made him feel a lot better.

"Aryan looks promising for a beginner." Anamika looked at Aryan and exchanged a smile with him as Bipasha joined her with a naughty smile.

Aryan started the manicure and by the time she was done with the anti-tanning mask, Aryan was applying the nail polish.

"I prefer the nudes." Anamika looked at him suggestively as Bipasha came to his rescue.

"Give the young man a break, madam. Anamika prefers the natural shades for her nail polish. She is an acclaimed social worker and a page three socialite. You will come to know more about her from the newspapers. Do not go by her jovial pranks that she is infamous for. She means no harm!" Aryan was relieved as the ragging got over on his first day at Aesthetics.

"Madam, do we go ahead with the pedicure as well?" Aryan had gained his confidence back as he offered the service.

"Bipasha, I told you that this young man has a lot of promise. He has already picked up the tricks of the trade. Yes, go ahead young man, and give my tired feet some real pleasure."

The two women laughed between them as Aryan got busy with readying his tools and apparatus to start the softening and the removal of calluses.

"Madam, considering your lifestyle, you must consider pampering yourself regularly. Regular facial will work wonders for your skin." Bipasha offered her advice while massaging her shoulders as Anamika surrendered herself for self-gratification. Aryan learnt about the black mud, fruit acids, vitamins, enzymes, gold, and the anti-oxidant range of facial services available at the salon. By the time they were done, Aryan had amassed a credible list of services. He was suitably impressed with Bipasha's tutoring while at work. She was an astute professional and great teacher!

"Here's something for you to have some fun Aryan." Anamika handed over a generous amount as a tip, winked at him and headed for the spa.

"This is your first tip, so you can keep it for yourself. The practice is to deposit the tip at the front office with Angela, who divides it among the entire team at the end of every business day." Aryan smiled at her and before he could ask her about his work, she looked at him appreciatively, which only meant that she was happy.

"I see a lot of promise in you, but now, go and get the next client. Let us get to paint some graying hairs."

Aryan happily obliged as he shot a question, "Bipasha, what do you mean by the tricks of the trade?"

"It is all about making the client spend the entire wallet in the salon. Do help him save some for the tip and the fare for his way back home. Your salary will get you the bread; it is the commission out of the sale and the tips that will get you the butter and the jam!" Bipasha laughed gaily as she gestured Aryan to escort the next client to the styling station.

On his way to the waiting lounge, Aryan noticed that one of the styling stations had a woman talking to a group of people. She was not shouting at anyone in particular, but sounded quite excited. While guiding the client towards Bipasha's styling station, he did not miss out in noticing Angela rushing towards the woman in action. Bipasha looked annoyed with the commotion around, but having realized that the client was already in her styling chair, she resumed with her charming talks. Aryan wanted to focus on the work at hand, but his curiosity got the better of him as he kept on looking at the group of people which was turning into a crowd.

"Aryan, let us start our work as you go ahead with the shampooing. Angela will talk to Nagma over there and everyone will be back to their work." Bipasha almost barked at Aryan in a stern voice, expressing her displeasure with the incidence that had taken place.

Aryan hurried with re-arranging the shampoo, conditioner, the hair straightening and perming kit, the styling gels, serum, mousse and the hair colours, before working out a rich lather for the client.

At lunch, the staff canteen was filled with excitement. The place that accommodated not more than six people at a time was crowded and had spilled over to the free passage just beside the canteen. Aryan and Bipasha walked towards the canteen and were taken aback with the resentment writ at large on the face of the staff that had trooped in.

"How do we carry on with this madness? There are clients waiting patiently at the lounge for their services and the entire salon seems to have thronged over here." Bipasha was talking all by herself.

"What is the matter?" Aryan asked.

Angela had reached the scene by then and asked for everyone's attention, "Madam is on her way and she wants all of you to be at your work stations. Roselyn will remain at the canteen along with the seniors."

"May I stay back with Roselyn so that she is comfortable?" Kanwal volunteered.

"Yes, I think you must stay back with her. Rest of you, disperse right now to attend the clients," Rehan, the god at Aesthetics spoke and no one dared to offer any other opinion. "Rana, let's go out for a smoke and wait till madam arrives to take control of the situation." Rehan asked Rana to accompany him outside for a smoke.

"Boss, Aryan has joined today. Let him come out with us so that you get to know each other better." Samir pulled

Aryan even before he could say anything and the four of them excused themselves to go outside.

Bipasha and Nagma stayed back in the canteen along with Roselyn and Kanwal for company. The crowd has started to thin down after Angela and Rehan gave them a piece of their mind. Peace prevailed temporarily at Aesthetics till Priya was to arrive to take charge of the situation.

The waiting lounge had a man sitting at a corner, shivering and panicking with bandages on his cheeks. There were two security guards keeping a close watch at him. The other people who were in the reception and the lobby were perplexed with the situation around, but upon learning the incidence that had transpired within the closed confines of the salon, they looked disgusted with the man. The reputation of Aesthetics was at stake and everyone was waiting for Priya.

The culprit was a man in his mid-forties, sporting expensive attire and a watch and was smelling of the chewing tobacco that he must be taking in plenty. Aryan took note of the man while going out of the salon with Rehan and others. The salon was back to its normal operations. Angela was frantically pacing the entire length and breadth of the salon. It helped her undermine the restlessness, but it also meant that she was anxiously waiting for the decision-maker.

"So, do you smoke?" Rana extended a cigarette towards Aryan.

"Yes, I do, but not now. Thank you for offering." Aryan shook his hands.

"Aryan has a timetable even for the petty vices." Samir chipped in with his idiocy but got stopped midway before he could continue further as Rehan looked at him threateningly.

"I am Rehan. Please do not take offence with Samir. He is the in-house comedian who provides all of us with welcome relief when we need it the most."

"No issues at all. I have been hearing so much about you from so many people that I am already in awe." Aryan looked at Rehan with genuine admiration, while he blew smoke rings in the air.

"Success is a relative term. The more successful you are, the greater the risk you carry in losing your crown to the next man in hiding," Rehan spoke with absolute contempt and it was well directed towards Rana, who was avoiding direct eye contact with him.

"I do not see anyone daring to think of snatching the crown, Rehan." Samir had to talk in between to prove his loyalty for Rehan.

"The followers are not necessarily your fans. You must not bother about the next man in hiding. It is the contender in waiting who must be giving you sleepless nights. But again, that should not bother you. You are a night rider and the city's night clubs will go out of business if you do not spend your nights over there." Rana chose his words pretty well. Sharp and incisive to make a point, but offend no one in particular.

Aryan could sense the profound impact of Rana's smart rebuttal as a brooding silence engulfed all of them.

"Hello Rana, I am Aryan."

"And, I presume you have not heard anything great about me as yet." Rana shook his hands and looked at him in anticipation of an acknowledgement.

"Well, today is my first day at Aesthetics and I am yet to know most of the people at the salon." Aryan was careful with his reply and it earned him a smile from the rest of the men.

"How do you know Priya madam?" Samir enquired.

"She was a counsellor and was responsible for assisting placements with the styling and grooming school from where I completed my certificate course."

"That explains you joining the salon as a stylist. But one must accept that she took the plunge and the net did appear. From being a mere counsellor to becoming the business head at Aesthetics, she must have played her cards right." Rana expressed doubts on her merit. He actually implied something considered to be normal with many men, when they find it difficult to accept a successful woman.

Aryan was privy to Priya's career graph, but he avoided discussing any further. While they got engrossed with discussing the incidence in the salon, a shiny Mercedes screeched to a halt and the two security guards rushed out to hold open the door. Clad in a white *salwar* and peach coloured *kameez*, it was Priya and she knew that the heads were turning. She took off the sun shades and her eyes caught Aryan at the corner with the others. She chose neither to acknowledge nor ignore him, for her eyes did the talking as she walked inside.

"Guys, let's go inside before we are summoned. And Samir, your jaws have dropped, get normal." All of them broke into an instant laughter as they followed Rehan inside the salon.

Roselyn's stint with Aesthetics and her stay in the city was still incomplete to teach her a lesson or two on how to fend off the wolves roaming in the open! She was the *Little Red Riding Hood* in the forest infested with the wolves. The wolves are always on the lookout for their prey, to be caught off the guard.

Roselyn was attending to this client for a facial treatment. The salon had the option between a curtained enclosure and the luxurious recliners in the open area for their customers. Normally, the lady customers availed the facial treatments in the enclosure while the men underwent their treatments in the open area. The client in question was being overtly patronizing and inquisitive about her, while she was preparing the applications.

Having chanced upon the fact that she hailed from the hills in Meghalaya, the man started regaling her with his fondness for the place. He, being a trader in fruits and spices visited the place quite often. Roselyn shed her initial inhibitions and became friendly with him with her conversation as the man proposed that they move inside the enclosure for the facial. He also assured her of availing the hair spa and the skin therapy. She was overjoyed at the prospect of earning a bounty as a commission from the sales. Roselyn accepted his proposal and took him inside the enclosure. The wolf emerged from the sheep's clothing!

"How much do I have to pay for a 'handshake'?" the man asked.

"You do not pay anything for a handshake," Roselyn replied innocently and extended her hand.

"You stay in the city all by yourself and it must be very lonely for someone like you to have left your home to stay among the unknown people. Give me your mobile number and we will plan a weekend. It will be an all expense paid trip to a luxurious resort. Satisfaction has a price tag, so quote me your price!" The wolf had started to trade between his lust and Roselyn's wide-eyed disgust. She was not someone to pander him for his indecent proposal.

"I cannot make anything of what you are proposing." She bravely countered him.

"Now, don't be a spoilsport. You agreed to the 'handshake' for free!" The brute started to unbutton when Roselyn gave a loud scream for help. Kanwal was in a recess, chatting with Nagma. He heard her scream and rushed to help her to catch the man with his pants down. He landed fierce blows on his face as he started bleeding profusely. Nagma was by Roselyn's side as she was shaking in rage, trying to recover from the disgusting encounter.

Priya was stunned to hear the detailed narrative from Nagma. Bipasha, Angela and Kanwal stood beside Roselyn as she tried to sober down.

"Madam, the man was bleeding after Kanwal beat him black and blue. The support staff has administered first aid on him. We were waiting for you to arrive and advice us on the way forward." Nagma had emerged as the spokesperson.

"But, we have a reputation to keep and the man happens to be a regular client. How about asking him to apologize? These kinds of incidences are rampant across most of the salons. We must also consider the fact that Roselyn was naïve to fall prey to his advances. She also broke the unwritten rule of taking the man inside the enclosure." Angela made her point.

"How can you talk like this Angela?" Kanwal thundered. "You are a woman and you are undermining the humiliation that Roselyn had to face from that beast. I think the man must be handed over to the police without sparing any further thought."

"I do not think that taking a step against the man will harm our reputation in any way. I would instead say that the clients will appreciate the fact that the management stood by Roselyn and that will be a positive endorsement for the salon besides instilling a sense of trust and respect for the women staff," Bipasha interjected with her perspective.

"Roselyn, what do you think that we must do?" Having heard each one of them with patience that the situation demanded, Priya went up to Roselyn, who was still sobbing. She did not answer anything at all as she threw herself at Priya, who consoled her in a tight hug. "Kanwal, please ask the security to get the man over here. He attempted at violating the sanctity of a woman. In all fairness, let us get to hear his side of the story as well," Priya asked Kanwal.

The security personnel got the man to the staff canteen. He was shivering from the excruciating pain of the severe beating from Kanwal, but was careful enough to feign ignorance when he pleaded for misunderstanding as the cause for the situation. "I am a regular customer. You can check my loyalty card and then you will realize the amount of money that you make out of me, every month. It is a case of misunderstanding and I think she did not understand my words in English and went ahead with creating a ruckus." The man was defiant and insisted upon protecting his own self.

Priya took the loyalty card from the man and threw it over to the garbage bin and then before anyone could make out what was coming next, she gave the man one tight slap across his face. The man was aghast as he held his hands over his face and fell to the floor. His face had turned red in utter humiliation. Roselyn got up from the chair and stood beside Priya and it was Angela's turn to rediscover the woman in her. She spit on him!

"The men of your upbringing salivate at any woman; they feast their eyes upon. You grope the breasts that feed you to grow up. You guys belong to a colony of vermin who will not think twice before groping your own mothers. You pigs thrive in the dark. I spoke to you in English and I think that there is no way you did not understand me, you rascal." The people in the room were getting to see Priya in a new avatar and they were glad to be working with her at Aesthetics.

The man was begging for mercy as everyone left him at the canteen with the security personnel keeping a watch.

Angela was at the front desk dialling the police. Priya noticed the appreciation in everyone's eyes as she walked out of the place. She was revered for the chair she occupied, but on that day, she won many hearts at Aesthetics, which also included the clients present. The only exception was Bipasha, who remained visibly unmoved with the entire episode involving Priya, and the high priestess did not miss out in noticing omission to the rule!

"Ok, everyone please get back to your business." Angela waved at the staff.

It had been close to six months that Aryan was working at the salon. Having successfully completed his stint in beauty and skin care under the guidance of Bipasha, he received a go-ahead from her to move under Rehan's tutelage. The first thing that struck Aryan while working with Rehan was his masterstroke with the combs and the brushes.

For someone uninitiated, like Aryan, to figure out the various combs and brushes was in itself one of the most laborious of all lessons. The square brush, two vent brush, rattail comb, wide toothed comb, paddle brush, rake hair brushes and combs! The list was exasperating and it took quite an effort from Aryan to get the names by rote and then try his hands with the application.

Rehan was not as easy to work with as Bipasha. Rehan was protective about sharing his proficiencies that had made him one of the brightest stars in styling and grooming. He made sure to park all of it in a 'no trespassing zone' as he appeared to be conspicuous with his insecurities. Aryan made futile attempts with befriending Samir at Rana's insistence to get closer to Rehan. Samir was too much in awe of his master to allow any invasion to his private space. All that mattered to him was not to jeopardize his own equation with Rehan.

Aryan broached the issue with Bipasha on a one-on-one basis, but she could not offer much headway with his problem. It was Nagma who asked him to take up the matter either with Angela, or better still, with Priya. Having thought over Nagma's advice over the days, he could not gather enough reason to approach Priya, which he thought could be seen as a petty matter to be brought to her notice. He decided to handle the problem himself, but he also knew from within that his hesitation to talk to Priya was unfounded.

After the incidence involving Roselyn, the entire salon had taken note of the fact that Kanwal had grown over-protective of her and she gave in to his vibes. The two were seen spending time together after working hours, enjoying each other's company. Rumour had it that Roselyn had already been to Kanwal's home on more than one occasion and the family approved their relationship.

In the meanwhile, Rana was working overtime to prove his mettle. He was gathering steam by regularly attending the training sessions and by walking an extra mile to win the trust and confidence of the clients. The results were visible as one could make out from the fact that Rana was counting almost the same amount as his commissions as Rehan from his work. His frequent breaks for smoking along with Rehan had reduced considerably, for he was gainfully engaged to the delight of the cash registers at the salon ringing incessantly.

In one of the instances, Samir tried to create a rift when he suggested to Aryan that with his increased visibility with the staff and the clients, Rana was getting edgy. Aryan made him irrelevant by ignoring his remarks and also made his presence feel unwelcome for his comfort. The good words from Nagma and the referrals from Bipasha were earning him the clients and that must have put Rehan in a tighter spot. It occurred to Aryan that it was about time that he took the matter to Angela. He wanted to work independently and he approached Angela in the canteen to discuss the same.

"Angela, I am wasting the salon's time and resources. Rehan is too busy with his work to take me under his wings. I think you must seriously consider my working independently." Aryan looked at Angela with a silent prayer in his lips.

"Aryan, you are not only good with the knives and scissors, but you speak well to make your point. I will talk to Rehan and you get ready to work independently from tomorrow." Angela had answered his prayers as he stood delighted.

"But, will Priya approve of it?"

"Nobody addresses madam by her first name, and you cannot be an exception," Angela cautioned him.

Aryan was conscious of making the mistake as he had gone a little too overboard with his prayer getting answered, but corrected himself immediately. "Sorry, it was unintentional."

"I will take her into confidence, provided you do not give any reason for the clients to complain."

"I owe you a treat, Angela."

"You owe me two! One for sharing madam's contact details when we met at the school, and I have just earned the other." Angela smiled at him and left for her work station.

At the close of the business hours for the day, Bipasha and Nagma congratulated him for having made it as an independent stylist. While descending the stairs from the salon, he saw Roselyn with Kanwal. "Congratulations Aryan! You have made it. Someday, I will become an independent stylist like you, and to begin with, I wish Angela makes me work with you as your assistant." Roselyn smiled at him and they rode off on the two-wheeler.

Aryan laughed all by himself as he was reminded of his dreams, where the hero always vanished with the woman of his dreams, on a two-wheeler!

Aryan took over as an independent stylist from the next day. He was fastidious with the gadgets and the tools, much to the agony of the support staff. He wanted the styling station to be spick and span. He ensured the carts and the trolleys were stocked with the hair clips, mixing bowls, water spray, paper towels, gloves, hair streamers and processors along with the hair dryers and the shampoo bowl. He took care to keep up with the trends to meet the demands of the customers. His strength was with the hair styling tools and the electronic grooming equipments. Be it the trimming scissors, the ridged curling iron, the big barrel curler, diffusers, the hot rollers and various other multi-styling kits.

He became an instant hit with the clients as an independent stylist. He was considered to be conversant with the latest trends and thus started earning the trust of his clients for his near perfect execution. It was the customised solution and the detailed discussions that followed in deciding the treatment, which became a hallmark of his service. The icing on the cake was, however, reserved for his ability to enter into any conversation with the client to make the entire experience get counted as a delightful affair.

Aesthetics had become a melting pot of human affairs. The clients appeared tight-lipped while waiting for their turn. But the moment they occupied their seat at one of the styling or therapy chairs, most of them became loose cannon balls exploding at the drop of a hat! Once the therapists started their application, comforting their pain points with their expert hand movements, they let go of their agonies and ecstasies embedded deep inside. Their embarrassments and regrets became a series of admissions. The salon doubled up as a rehabilitation of the bruised minds where they found the best of listeners.

The lonely wife of an engineer in the merchant navy ruminating upon the absence of her life partner for most of the time during the year, but wanting to retain her best looks for the husband to admire, once he came back from sailing the high seas. A fading star of the silver screen, singing own paeans of the heightened glory of his stardom, once achieved but remembered by no one. The childless couple, deciding the therapy for one another to inscribe one of the better love stories that would never get written. The lady doctor refusing to take her calls for she knew that the patient was about to breathe his last. The high paid professional in the private sector, not wanting to accept the fact that he had become a liability for the organisation.

The epiphanies in Aryan's life were his biggest source for the conversations!

The city was reeling under the sweltering heat of the hot summer sun when one day, the monsoon clouds announced their arrival. It started to pour. The rains came with a lot of promise to quench the thirst of many insatiable souls.

Aryan was occupied with applying a rich brown hair dye on a client when one of the support staffs informed him that he had a visitor. He was surprised, but finished his job at hand before taking off the apron and heading towards the reception. It was Reema. She was withdrawn from the surroundings, as she was occupied with a magazine in her hands. She was wearing reading glasses and looked very dignified in her traditional attire.

"Reema, what brings you here?" Aryan was too happy to find the right expressions and the words for the situation as he was meeting her after a long time.

She kept the magazine aside, rose up from the chair to walk up to him as she handed over an envelope.

"What is this?" Aryan enquired, as he opened the envelope without waiting for her reply.

It was the advice from the Union Public Service Commission, advising her to join the National Academy of Administration, Mussoorie. She had cleared the civil services examination!

"Bhaiya, my preparation for the civil services was a meditation in seeking penance for all my wrong doings. My parents encouraged me to continue my studies and the subsequent preparation for the civil services after I left Rohan." Reema's face was gleaming with pride while her eyes were moistened with remorse.

"I am so proud of you." Aryan tried to hold back his tears.

"Bhaiya, I have decided to file for divorce. I think both of us have to give ourselves a fresh lease of life as individuals."

"I will not ask you to reconsider your decision. I will pray for your happiness." Aryan patted on her back.

"I will take your leave today, but I will come back to meet you after I have completed my training." Reema assured him and was about to leave when something occurred to Aryan.

"How did you find me?" he asked her.

"I had been to the earlier address and met up with Kavya and Arvind. They helped me with the address of your new house, where your landlord gave me the address of this salon."

"You met Kavya and Arvind?" It sounded more of a dramatic surprise than a mere question.

"Yes, I met the two of them together. They are running a pre-school chain and looked happy with each other." Reema handed a business card to Aryan as he guided her out of the salon.

He was happy for Reema and also felt relieved for Kavya and Arvind after what they must have been through in their lives.

The business card read 'Ms. Kavya Srivastava – Franchisee, Bright Kids'.

The political establishment was just about managing to govern the country, which was getting divided along caste and religious lines. The government claimed to be making significant progress in eliminating the historical blunders of the past. Stronger alliances were getting forged with the global majors to promote trade relationships, the renewal of diplomatic ties and meaningful strategic partnerships.

The opposition kept lambasting the government on failing to deliver the promises on employment, price rise and economic growth. The government made counter claims that the opposition was disrupting the parliamentary proceedings to stall the federal structure and the democratic fabric of the country. The opposition kept on experimenting with their coalition partners, but drew blanks to the delight of the government in power, which kept on winning one state election after the other. While the dynastic hegemony of the grand old political party remained unchallenged, the incumbent government started setting the precedence of idol worshiping of the king maker and the King.

Each and every event in the country started getting politicized for petty electoral gains. The media got divided between the prime time elite erudite and mouth pieces for the hoi polloi. Fake news surfaced with the material evidence of their political sponsorships. After the initial short-lived popularity, it went on to earn immense disrepute for having influenced the people with bogus claims, which was passed off as news.

The structural changes in exercising fiscal prudence with respect to uniform taxation and streamlining the parallel economy by eliminating black money sent a shiver down the spine of the corrupt and the non-compliant. The biometric policing through a central data mining exercise for various social welfare schemes got launched one after another till it got branded as the means for attaining political appeasement of the targeted beneficiaries.

New and young faces emerged in the national politics to champion the cause of the socially backward classes. However, they got sucked into the mainstream politics to join either the government or the opposition to address their personal agenda. Interesting terminologies started getting coined, racing to find a place in the dictionary. Three distinct categories of opinions got demarcated between the left-winged liberals, the moderates without wings and the right-winged extremists. The latest sensation in the state was Raghav Tiwari who had grabbed the headlines for switching over his political loyalty, after the debacle around the chit fund scam involving RGV Enterprises. It was assumed that his political patrons would have allayed his fears with the dreaded investigations of the central agencies.

The court kept conducting the fair trial while the judicial commission started working overtime to compensate losses, and Raghav kept on laying the foundation stones of his political party at the grass root levels. The target was to turn the tide in favour of his new political affiliation. The people who had counted losses out of the scam started accepting the fact that it was predestined and went about with their lives as usual.

Rhea was leaving no stones unturned at the studios in New Delhi. She had become a newscaster by then and was working towards claiming the prime-time slot. But she was losing the firm grounds of the professional conduct to the impunity enjoyed by a handful of people who belonged to a rare school of thought. This creed of journalism believed in dishing out spicy items in the disguise of news. The survival of the news channel was dependent upon dishing out juicy content and saucy controversies.

Rohan was languishing in the jail, counting his days. He had received the notice for divorce from Reema through her lawyer and he had chosen to go ahead with closing the chapter forever. He did not regret the fact that no one from his family ever paid a visit to him in jail. He had toughened himself with the impending isolation that he anticipated when he would be out from the prison.

Rohan's only hope with Aryan, who according to him was an emotional fool meant to be exploited on any given day. He had no other plans but to seek refuge under Aryan and chart his future course of action. There was still no news about their mother. Aryan carried on with remaining busy with his work and had very little time for himself.

The gated community which had sprung up at the place which was once a home to Aryan and his family was partially occupied. Most of the apartments were on rent. Faced with litigation issues and the non-compliance of statutory requirements, Raghav had turned a blind eye to the residents. Most of the amenities that were promised as a part of the venture never got delivered.

The housing project was considered to be a curse and the people in the neighbourhood attributed it to Raghav's ill-gotten wealth at the expense of the poor. But whenever Aryan crossed the place, he knew it was the wrath of a woman wronged, for she never got back her home to stay with her children.

Gitanjali was keeping pace with the change in the social order that came with the usual unrest for some time, but to gradually settle down and get accepted as normal. The society at large was experiencing a behavioral pattern which defied logic but suited the policy makers. The money was moving from the immovable assets to the financial assets. The fall in the real estate prices, low interest rate in the bank's deposits, consistent rise in the price of fuel and commodities coupled with the maddening demand for services and consumables had become a part of life. The society was learning to embrace disruptive practices.

The beauty and the health care industry was flourishing and became one of the front runners in generating employment and business opportunities. Aesthetics kept on adding the outlets one after another to an already invincible list of their market dominance.

Rehan retained his pole position at the salon, but he was getting discussed more for his exploits after the business hours. Samir's proximity with Rehan had earned him handsome dividends as he had started to ride a sparkling bike to his work. Kanwal and Roselyn were happy with each other for company, and were believed to be tying the nuptial knot very soon. Rana was emerging as the worthy contender for the crown, to be seriously considered as a lead stylist, while Bipasha made her intentions public. She was ready to start her own with Karan Seth as the investor in her beauty and wellness business. Angela was duty-bound to keep Priya posted of the developments at the master outlet to earn her extra brownie points.

In one of those usual mornings, Nagma entered the salon with an exceptional exuberance. She proudly shared the news of her brother having completed his MBBS degree. The entire staff of the twenty odd people in the salon congratulated the jubilant sister as she announced a grand biriyani party on the following day. She would cook it by herself and assured everyone of the *firni* to round up the feast at the staff canteen! It was one accomplishment in the waiting for far too long for Nagma that gave her a purpose in life and a life for a purpose to her ailing father.

In was raining heavily since the morning. Aryan gave his morning walk a miss for the day as it took some time for him to drag himself out of the bed. He made tea for himself and went to the window. He noticed the partially soaked newspaper that hung in the door. A pair of pigeons had conveniently perched themselves in the external unit of an air conditioner.

The street children were out on the road, enjoying every bit of the rainfall. They were unmindful of their compatriots who were forced to remain inside their house under the watchful eyes of their parents. The rickshaw pullers were out to make the best of bargains as the harrowed office going crowd was ready to shell out a princely sum for the rickshaw ride in the rains. It was the toll for toil on a rainy day!

Aryan initially thought of giving his work a miss, but then he knew that Nagma was hosting the feast for the entire staff at the salon, to celebrate her brother's achievement. The salon had become a family to many of them. Not turning up at work would be playing spoilsport to the woman's hope of getting her family members by her side. Aryan went about getting ready for the day.

It was a weekday and the salon was nearly empty when Aryan walked in. The staff was turning up one after another for their work, much later than their usual time. The lounge was sporting a neat look and the attendants looked relieved with very little work around. Nagma was the first to arrive and she had personally attended to the office along with the support staffs in converting the staff canteen into a makeshift banquet.

Angela was at her workstation, checking the attendance and the appointments. She started issuing orders to the support staff to get ready and spring into action. The rains had by then decided to hold back its rage as it started to drizzle. It was close to noon when clients started to arrive at Aesthetics. The salon was ready for clients to breathe life upon their arrival, as they started getting assigned to the styling stations.

The staff canteen was filled with the soulful aroma of spices and the condiments and the clients could not help but notice the eagerness of the staff to wait for the clock to strike for the lunch time! Angela had already made an exception for the day. She had the necessary permissions in place to organise the lunch for the entire staff together at the lunch time. The clock struck one and the team ran down!

Nagma had laid the food on the table. She was blending the saffron coloured basmati rice in the two big food containers, which was overflowing with the sumptuous delight known as the biriyani. Another container lay beside the biriyani with the sautéed light brown potatoes and eggs, a specialty that makes the Kolkata Biriyani as one of the most admired dishes. She was thoughtful enough to have got some crispy *lachcha parathas* along with *malai kofta* for the vegetarians among the staff. Roselyn and Bipasha were helping her arrange the firni in small plastic cups. The staff canteen was effortlessly converted into a banquet with the greedy eyes and the gluttonous tongues salivating at the prospect of the awesome food!

"We have an hour to relish the food and then disperse." Angela served herself, as she issued the orders.

A queue was formed as Nagma, Roselyn and Bipasha started serving the food. The atmosphere was festive and people had to be coaxed to make way for others to get their plateful of pleasure!

"Nagma, here's something we got for your brother. Bipasha & I bought this yesterday on behalf of the entire team." Roselyn handed her a wristwatch, cologne and a backpack as a gift for her brother. Nagma had tears in her eyes that sparkled with pride and gratitude as the entire team clapped.

"Who has the best camera phone? Let's capture this rare moment." Samir pulled everyone closer while Kanwal and Rana took photographs, interchanging the roles as smart phone photographers.

"I am touched, you all are my family." Nagma thanked everyone as they continued with the feast.

"So, the party is on! Congratulations Nagma," Rehan announced his arrival.

Nagma smiled at him.

"I am a vegetarian and there are some others as well," Samir casually interjected, to which Nagma did not reply as she served him the vegetarian plate to his surprise.

"The *great barrier beef* has already divided the country. I have been careful to not take any chances in raking any controversy with the food." Nagma was unnerved with Samir's failed attempt at stirring a discomfort with the food.

"I find it amusing that the food and the eating habits are identifying and deciding the nationalist from a traitor."

Bipasha tucked in the chicken biriyani and added her bit of wisdom to the discussion.

"I have realized that our surname is the basis of the prejudice. As long as we are on the first name basis, we have no room for being judgmental. The moment we use our surnames, a clear divide surfaces up as perceptions and bias overtake our rationale." Nagma had the audience listening to her with rapt attention.

"Why do you say that? What is my identity without my surname?" Rana asked her.

"Nagma Qureshi, Rehan Ali, Samir Yadav, Rana Mishra, Bipasha Dutta, Roselyn Shylla, Kanwaljeet Singh and Aryan Roy Chowdhury are the names and now we all know them by their religion. This knowledge has created the divide. The cognizance is given to our religion, caste, the eating habits and the political ideology, associated with our names. Our full name is no longer our identity, but a matter of crisis!" Nagma spoke with such articulation that people around her started wondering if they would ask for one more helping of the food or remain glued to her oratory skills.

"Has it ever occurred to you that I am not welcome as your neighbour and you will never reside in our ghetto?" Rehan did not complain but he seemed to be justifying the pains of being considered unwelcome.

"I will not agree with what you say Rehan. After the partition, the governments in succession have been creating a social fabric of inclusive growth, which includes education, health, infrastructure and employment. Since you chose to remain in the dark, you got counted as nothing more than a vote bank," Rana countered Rehan's justification.

"As a member of the minority community, you opted to enjoy mostly the privileges. The political system in the country found it convenient to take up your issues only when you mattered, during the elections. You felt good that someone was taking up your cause, which remained an empty promise long after you voted them to power. Why do you think that the representation from your community in the bureaucracy, administration, defense, science and technology etc., is considered to be a mockery of the level playing field? I think it is because you never wanted to forego the privileges, because you think you are entitled to it." Rana shared his thought-provoking perspective and then focused on the food.

"He has a point, Rehan. Most of the politicians in our country have survived only because of the caste and religious divide. We have rarely exercised our rights as the citizen to ask for education, health, sanitation and employment opportunities. This has resulted in a trust issue between the communities." Nagma found sense in Rana's point of view.

"After so many years of independence, it is amusing that we still get to hear about the need to eradicate illiteracy, but there is no minimum educational qualification required to get voted to power!" Kanwal made his point as Roselyn looked at him admiringly.

"The illiterates and blood-sucking politicians want us to remain illiterate so that we do not question them. The common people like us remain occupied with earning a living and paying the taxes." Aryan was known to be a reticent man, but when he spoke, he got heard.

"Most of the politicians of different ideologies ridicule our righteousness by celebrating together in their backyards, every time we get divided over religious and caste-based issues. Have you ever heard of a politician, a priest, a pundit or a maulvi getting killed in a riot? They are the vultures who get fed and flourish as long as we remain divided." Aryan drilled a lot of sense in the gathering.

The group had started to thin off by then as some of the staff could hardly make any sense of the discourse and thus, they went back to their duties after profusely thanking Nagma for the feast.

"I am glad that we are discussing these contentious issues. When I came to this city, I had faced a different kind of isolation. People were just not willing to take me as a paying guest or as a tenant. You all are discussing divide on religious lines? Let me tell you how ignorant and insensitive are the people from the mainland towards their own countrymen who hail from the Northeastern states." The soft-spoken Roselyn broke the barriers that she had imposed upon herself.

"What made the man make an indecent proposal to me? It is because most of you want to believe that we are aliens in our own country. You differentiate us on the basis of looking different. Our easy-going lifestyle and the innocence that you notice in us makes us vulnerable to most of you being cunning. It makes the majority of people think that we can be exploited and are easily available. In your case it is a matter of trust, and in our case, it is a matter of honour!" Roselyn echoed the voice of the people from the distant hills in the Northeastern states of India, and it put everyone to shame.

As everyone was getting ready to leave the canteen, it was Angela's turn to account for the discretions and discernment faced by the already dwindling Anglo-Indian community in the city. Angela was always tightlipped about herself, in maintaining a dignified silence over her insecurities, but then, finding her colleagues talk so freely in addressing issues that concerned each one of them, she decided to come out with her pronouncement.

"I must admit that I have always kept my fears of seclusion hidden in my straight face. I know many of you laugh at my back and avoid being friends with me, because you think that I am nothing more than a stooge. If you think that beef and pork has divided the country, then people in my community are living in a no man's land. Everybody considers us to be rank outsiders and most of you think that we cannot be anything more than being a receptionist or an ageing personal secretary. The most despicable part is that even the films have been stereotyping our community in a similar way," Angela spoke at length and the stillness that ensued, pricked the conscience of all those who were present in the canteen.

"Hello everyone, the celebration is becoming too cerebral for all of us to have enjoyed the awesome food. After all the discussions on meat, I wish I could become a non-vegetarian for a day." Everyone broke into instant laughter as Samir went for the third helping of the firni. Kanwal sought everyone's attention with Roselyn by his side.

"We have some happy news to share with you all. Our families have agreed to the marriage and I will be quitting the salon to join my family business. You all are invited and I will be handing you a formal invite shortly," Kanwal's announcement brought another round of cheer as Roselyn turned pink, blushing with pride.

"Will Roselyn continue to work or she becomes a pretty face at home?" Samir asked.

"That's for her to decide, but I think she would love to continue over here," Kanwal put an end to the discussion once and for all.

"Each one of us has a sob story to tell. I feel so light that I could share my story with you all. Now, let us get back to our work. The rains have stopped and the lounge is abuzz with activities." Angela got everyone grounded to the reality and stepped forward to help Nagma to clean the place as Bipasha and Roselyn joined them along with some of the support staff.

Countless Epiphanies

Aryan was growing restless with each passing day with no news about his mother. Staying alone in the house was becoming a nightmare. His only hope was with Rohan joining him after he got released from the prison so that they could stay together in the place. After the divorce from Reema and in the absence of their mother at home, Aryan knew that Rohan would need a moral pillar for support.

Aryan had earned his share of repute at the salon with close to one year of his being with Aesthetics. He counted a steady list of clientelle who were enamoured by his conversations while availing the services. It was a sort of a revelation to the staff at large, as Aryan otherwise preferred to keep a reserved distance from most of the people. Kanwal had left the salon but was regular to pick up Roselyn after work, to drop her at the paying guest accommodation.

Rana was fiercely advancing towards the pole position as a stylist as Rehan was noticeably losing his grip with the regular clients. The salon was rife with rumours that he had succumbed to substance abuse. Interestingly, Samir was losing his comic timings, which was otherwise considered to be a welcome relief for the staff from the monotony of the work load and was often found to be gloomy during the work hours. Rehan had humiliated him on more than one occasion and Samir was quite upset with the change in his equation with Rehan.

One day while Aryan was giving the finishing touches to a client, Nagma came to him with a request to accommodate one of the regular clients with the salon, beyond his other appointments. "Rehan has not reported for work today and he had not informed Angela about it. The appointment could not get re-scheduled as the client has already dropped at the designated slot for the services. Bipasha & I are already expected to work overtime with the additional load."

"In which case, I do not have a choice but to attend to the client when you all are sharing the extra load." Aryan's words comforted Nagma as she introduced Ahana to Aryan for the hair treatment at the spa, followed by a haircut.

"How long are you with Aesthetics? I don't seem to have noticed you," Ahana's voice belied her pretty looks as she spoke with distinct command.

"I am working here for more than a year now. I learnt that Rehan attends to you but he has not reported for work today." Aryan was polite with opening the conversation, but their eyes did not meet properly as he was busy with arranging the styling station for the services.

"I do not remember having settled for anything less than the best in my life. I was not aware that Rehan will not be around today. Else, I would have rescheduled my appointment. Tell me something, Nagma looked out for Rana and Bipasha before recommending you to me. Is this the pecking order of preference for a specialist over here?" Ahana was sharp with her dismissal for Aryan as a substitute for Rehan.

Aryan turned at her and their eyes met. "Nagma is a senior stylist over here and she would not want you to settle for anything less than the best. Aesthetics is renowned to pamper the clients and the fact that Nagma chose to recommend me to you, confirms that you are too invaluable a client to be lost." Aryan was in his immaculate act of using the precise words for the situation.

"You speak too well for a stylist." Ahana was disarmed with his self-confidence.

"You compliment too well to be a discerning client yourself."

They looked at each other and a conspiracy got hatched instantly to make a match between the two adorable hearts!

"I will go for the hair spa to begin with and then I leave it to your expert eyes to decide upon a contemporary hair style." Ahana let go of her initial reservations and settled down for the hair spa.

"Can I offer you some beverage while we get ready for the services? The best of the clients prefer the fruit mocktail over tea and coffee." Aryan had cast a magical spell as he went to fetch her beverage. Ahana was caught in the web and she did not complain.

"I think you must consider the hair length till your shoulder level. It will go very well with your slender frame to highlight the back as I will work out layers and depth to the hair and it will look flattering on you." Aryan held her hair on his hands while suggested the hair style.

"That sounds more of a personal preference than a professional advice." Ahana attempted at being a wisecrack to catch him off his guards.

"As a trained stylist, we are taught not to exercise any personal remark or opinion for our clients. But, in your case I am making an exception because my personal preference and the professional advice seem to be agreeing with each other." Aryan was too much in control to get unnerved by the sudden jibe drawn at him.

"Do you indulge in these flirtatious attempts with all your lady clients or you are again making an exception?" Ahana was getting her hair air-dried after the hair spa as she got up from the chair to settle down before the grand mirror. She noticed Aryan looking at her in the mirror as they spoke to each other.

"I am willing to risk my professional repute for the first time," said Aryan.

"What if I deter you from taking any further steps?"

"Had that been the case, you would not have put up this question to me?"

"You are definitely not a novice with the choice of your words with a woman. We hardly know each other and you are already making advances with your client?" Ahana teased him.

"I would not have dared if I had not noticed the flutter in your eyes and the tremble in your voice. You are almost whispering to me right now, instead of creating a ruckus as a client who has been offended." Aryan delivered a knockout punch with his carefully chosen words.

A support staff arrived at the scene to remove the mocktail glass and to assist Aryan with arranging the hair cutting tools and gadgets. The young lad's arrival got the two of them back to their senses from the dreamlike world as they got conscious of his presence.

"I will go for the hair style that you wish for me." Ahana broke the uneasy calm.

"Thank you for granting my wish and here we go." Aryan signalled the assistant to leave and asked him to join them once they were done with the haircut, only to continue the conversation.

"How come you ended up being a stylist over here?" asked Ahana.

"You seem to be in no mood to compromise your quest for the best?"

"Why do you say so? I do not mean to intrude into your personal space. I am just plain curious to know what made you opt for this career when most of the people of our age are into so many other things like software, BPO and engineering, etc."

Aryan felt comfortable to come across the reassuring voice in Ahana as he went about narrating the transformation of a man with average academic abilities to become a stylist at Aesthetics. He shared his deep regrets of having misunderstood a sensitive man in his father and the disturbing fact that his mother had gone missing for more than a year. He was ecstatic to share Rhea's feat but agonized with sharing Rohan's misdeeds. He chose to leave out the entire chapter on Kavya, not because he wanted to avoid being truthful, but to respect the sanctity of their friendship.

By the time he was through with recounting the facts of his life, Ahana's hair styling got over. She stood in front of the mirror and could not help admit that she was flattered with the hair style as she handed over her business card.

"No tips for sharing the amazing story of your life till date. We must meet very soon as you have to hear out my fairy tale!" Ahana exchanged the contact coordinates with Aryan and they promised each other to meet very soon.

Soon after she had left, Aryan felt somewhat secured of the possibilities that could emerge out of their meeting each other. He remembered Priya's words of wisdom on the day they met at the RGV mall when she was about to be taken into custody. She had advised Aryan to quit living the life of a hermit and start discovering a life for him.

Aryan felt relieved with a newly bolstered self-assurance after finding someone in whom he had confided upon the entire book on his life. A peculiar sense of feeling wanted and the fact that he mattered to someone, made him feel very special. The fact that Ahana heard him out and wanted to meet him again, gave him a new purpose with life. Aryan was finding it difficult to concentrate on his work and it became apparent that his mind was meandering in the meadows of eternal happiness that could no longer chain him to the walls in the salon. He decided to leave early for the day and went to seek Angela's approval for the same.

"Angela, I want to leave early as I do not feel like working," Aryan said.

"Is everything fine with you? We are already short on staff, but I will not insist upon your staying back if you are not feeling well." Angela showed genuine concern for Aryan as he had never sought a break from work, but for the weekly leave and the public holidays.

Nagma rushed to Aryan's rescue. "Don't worry Angela, we will manage between us. The young man seems to be smitten by someone special." Nagma smiled at Aryan naughtily, but he took no offence of her friendly tease and thanked her for coming to his rescue to leave the salon for the day.

Aryan decided to walk back home. He longed to be in Ahana's company. He took out her business card, flicked it many a time before forcing himself not be abrupt with calling her up. He also felt stupid with himself in having allowed the people back at the salon to easily notice him getting fidgety. But he also enjoyed the attention only to realize that he had developed a soft corner for Ahana!

The honking of a car at the traffic signal got him back to his senses. A convoy of cars was escorting someone important enough to have brought the traffic to a complete standstill. Aryan caught a glimpse of Raghav in one of the cars, trailing the dignitary visiting the city as a passerby cheekily remarked. "What a nightmare for the minister! He is beating a hasty retreat. The state government must have rejected the central government's new policy on taxes." Aryan wasted no further time in getting involved in discussing and debating political designs. He knew that the opinion of the masses did not matter.

He deliberately took the road that took him through the place that once housed his family. The place looked ghostly, abandoned by most of the occupants after losing out their patience of not getting the basic amenities that were promised by Raghav when they purchased their flats in the gated community.

Aryan had no animosity towards any of them. He actually could relate to their miseries of having been cheated by Raghav who was moving scot free, while the inhabitants must be running from pillar to post in seeking a solution for their grievances. He thought of the checklist that he had once created along with Rhea to fight back with Raghav, but now he had accepted having lost the battle. He laughed out loud at the brazenness of his challenge, which he had once posed for Raghav.

Aryan kept walking and crossed the place where he had spent a considerable time of his life. A bright glow sign board of the 'Bright Kids' playschool on the ground floor had lit up the garden and Aryan could see the flowers that were once tended by an elderly man, now blooming. The house was blessed again by becoming an abode for a couple who had already braved a lot of odds in their married life, but had decided to give their relationship another chance.

It was late in the evening by the time Aryan reached his home. Someone was sitting on the steps leading to the house.

The silhouette was recognizable and it increased his heartbeat as he picked up pace. He fumbled for the house keys as he stumbled upon the man!

"Rohan, how long have you been waiting over here?" He gently picked up Rohan from the steps and led him inside the house.

Aryan handed him a glass of water and sat beside him on the bed. Rohan drank the water, got up from the bed and went to the table to pour some more water. "Bhaiya, I am sorry for getting all the misfortunes for the family. Reema had come to the prison along with her lawyer to get the signatures for the divorce. I learnt about Ma going missing and that you have changed the house. She gave me this address," Rohan spoke in a single breath.

"Rohan, go to the bathroom and freshen up while I cook us the dinner." Aryan showed him around the house and handed him some fresh clothes. Rohan rushed inside to cleanse himself of the dirt, soil and his sins! While having the dinner, Aryan observed Rohan weeping as tears ran down his cheeks, but he chose to ignore his repentance. It was a part of his reparation to realise the preciousness of one lifetime. It is a gift, not to be squandered!

"Hello Rhea, is it a good time to talk to you?" Aryan had dialled up her number.

"Yes bhaiya, it has been quite some time that we spoke with each other. I had a tough day today and I wanted to be among my own. I am glad that you called up."

"Rhea, were you ever angry enough with Rohan to completely sever your ties with him?"

"Bhaiya, it is one umbilical cord that ties the three of us. I am upset with him as he was the most promising among us. I have my resentment with him on what he did to himself and his relationships. But I cannot disown him as my brother." Rhea was being candid as Aryan posed her with a surprise.

"What would you do if you get to speak with him right now?"

"I would take him in my arms, cry upon his shoulder and plead with him to reform his life. I know he is with you and he is feeling awkward to talk to me. Please pass on the phone to him."

What followed during the next few minutes was nothing short of a dramatic reunion of the siblings. Rohan was crying inconsolably over the phone, begging for an apology. Aryan took over the phone from Rohan and spoke to Rhea who was sobbing at the other end.

"Rhea, I happen to pass by our own house today and I have accepted our fate that we have lost the house forever. I think the time has come for us to consolidate our lives hereafter."

"What about Ma? I have tried all my professional resources to find her, but to no avail. I am worried that either the police have given up on her or we have started believing that she is longer alive." Rhea admitted her deepest fears as she spoke with Aryan.

"First things first, let us try to do something for Rohan and then we will make one final attempt with locating our mother." Aryan was the man in the house as he knew that his siblings wanted to be comforted by him at that moment.

"You are right, bhaiya. Ask Rohan not to lose heart and that we are together in this battle." Rhea always had the dominant traits of their mother and her resilience reinforced it once again.

Aryan hung up the phone and took the couch while Rohan slept on a mattress on the floor. The calmness of the night with his brother in the house made Aryan feel relaxed. His eyes became drowsy and dreams came to him after a long time. He watched his father reading him the letter that he had come across after his father's death. His head was on his mother's lap and then he caught a pretty woman on a bike. He did not regret this time as Ahana was riding at the back of a glitzy bike with Aryan and they drove away happily.

Aryan woke up in the morning to Rohan's call. He had prepared tea for Aryan. Rohan had lost a lot of weight and looked older to his age. Aryan looked at him and remembered that it was the same Rohan who had once drilled considerable sense in his head for a career. Today, Aryan was a sought-after stylist in the most prominent salon chain in the country.

"Rohan, you stay back at home. Let me meet some people to find out some work for you." Rohan nodded in agreement to his brother's advice. Aryan called up Ahana.

"Hello Ahana, how are you placed during the day?"

"Good morning Aryan. I have some light work and then completely occupied after lunch. What is the matter?"

"Can we meet up?"

"Aryan, we just got acquainted yesterday and you are already rushing up. I am not very comfortable with the idea."

"Ahana, it is about my brother Rohan. He has come home and I was wondering if we could meet up sometime during the day so that you could help me with some ideas; as I need to find out some meaningful engagement for him."

"Aryan, come over to my place. I work out of home. We can meet at 10.30 a.m. today."

"I am not known to your family. Will it be right for me to drop in unannounced at your place?"

"Aryan, I meet my clients and business associates at home. You are coming over to discuss Rohan and not to ask for my hand in marriage." Aryan got her message, took the address and got moving.

The two-storied house, styled as a bungalow in the posh locality stood out in the crowd with its freshly painted exterior walls. Aryan had no difficulty in finding the address. A man, who was most possibly the gardener, opened the gates to the bungalow. An elderly couple was reading the newspapers over their tea. They looked up at the stranger and enquired about his landing at their place.

"Good morning, I am Aryan. I have an appointment with Ahana." The couple nodded without uttering any word as the gardener led him inside the house.

Ahana was in the drawing room, waiting for him to show up. Having heard Aryan speak at length on Rohan's academic background and his work experience, Ahana realized that she had nothing much to offer. "Aryan, I am a postgraduate in contemporary literature and I work as a curator for information and knowledge on various subjects for my clients, who primarily run web-based businesses. I have never worked in any professional organisation and thus feel genuinely challenged to offer any solution for Rohan at this moment." Ahana was candid with her limitations. The coffee and the cookies arrived in the drawing room as she continued with the discussion.

"My father has retired from his work very recently. He worked in a senior capacity with the central government. I will talk to him and find out if he can be of any help. He has a very influential network of friends and colleagues. But I will not promise anything to you as I am not sure if he would do something for a stranger."

"That will be very helpful. I must now take your leave." Aryan got up to leave.

"I did mention to you that I have light work till the lunch time. You must meet my parents. I am asking you to have lunch with us."

"It is really nice of you to ask a stranger over for lunch. I am already feeling uneasy for having asked you to help me for my brother. I must now take your leave." Aryan sounded embarrassed.

"Aryan, you would have made a remarkable sprinter. You are always in a rush to finish the race. I am asking you to join us over lunch so that you do not remain a stranger for my parents! You relax over here while I go and inform my parents that you are joining us over for lunch." Ahana was ruthless with her words and she had Aryan wanting for more! He looked at her in absolute wonder. She was prevailing over him since the time they had met and during every instance, when he thought that he had outwitted her.

Ahana's parents were graceful hosts and made him feel comfortable in their company. Ahana's father was a gregarious gentleman and took no time to befriend Aryan. Her mother was a social worker and she wrote poems in her leisure. Aryan shared all possible details about his family and his work.

"I am so glad that you spoke honestly with my parents. I have known them to be progressive in their outlook and they respect people for who they are and not what they could have become. I think we must give time to one another to find out if we would be compatible in a long-term relationship." Ahana took the lead in their relationship as Aryan thanked her for the lunch.

"Ahana, you are blessed to have such a wonderful family and I am glad that you insisted upon my staying over for the lunch. The three of you make a beautiful picture frame."

"There are actually *four* of us in the family. My elder brother is currently overseas. He will be visiting us during Durga Puja. I must warn you beforehand that he is too protective about me. If you can win him over, which is nothing short of baptism by fire, I see no reason why the two of us cannot tango for a lifetime!"

They laughed heartily till they were interrupted by a phone call from Kanwal. "Aryan, I had come over to the salon to invite you to our marriage reception. I am leaving the invitation card with Angela. You must come along with others to join us in our happiness."

"Congratulations Kanwal, I am so happy for you and Roselyn. I will definitely come over to the reception." Aryan took Ahana's leave and took a cab to home.

Rohan took unusually long to answer the doorbell, which got Aryan worried till he noticed Rohan struggling to keep his eyes open. In the evening, they went to the local market for shopping clothes and utilities for Rohan and then dropped at Jeevan's food joint. Having placed their orders, Aryan got busy with observing the crowd, with a faint hope to find someone known to him.

Rohan was struggling to decide what to go for first, but then, gradually started relishing the entire spread of the food. He belched out after finishing the food, completely indifferent to the people making faces at his uncouth conduct as he looked shyly at Aryan. "Bhaiya, the food is heavenly. I could not stop myself from eating all of it."

Aryan took out the money as he replied to him, "Rohan, it is not about the food. The food we take at home is mundane. Jeevan knows it very well that we come to this place to taste the spice with the food. Look at his success story of finding the right spices for the food. We are gladly paying up for it without any complains."

"Bhaiya, you are a changed man." Rohan looked at him with a respect in his eyes.

"Let us spice up our lives and be ready to pay a price for it." Aryan put his hands around his brother's shoulders and started walking back home. He shared his very recent acquaintance with Ahana and her family. Rohan was glad that his brother and Ahana were taking measured steps in their relationship.

The Fridays are the dry days at Aesthetics as the bulk of the appointments get booked for the weekends. It was a mere coincidence that Roselyn and Kanwal's marriage reception was on a Friday. Kanwal's family had spared no efforts in throwing a gala reception. The big reception area hosting a large number of invitees was adorned with exotic flowers and silky coloured drapes.

The live entertainment counter which is typical of the Punjabi weddings was keeping the guests on their feet as they were breaking into spontaneous dance to the *bhangra* beats. The sprawling open area, right in the middle of the mansion was pulling the highest number of invitees over the live barbeque counters and the makeshift bar, where the liquor was being served in plenty.

The newly wedded couple was standing picture perfect at the corner of the lawn and was too happy to oblige the selfie hunters and the family for group photographs. The groom's parents were exchanging pleasantries and formally introducing the extended family and the guests to Roselyn's parents who had chosen to remain seated at a corner, overawed with the lavishness of the affair. Roselyn and Kanwal rushed towards their colleagues, the very moment they were spotted entering the venue. After the perfunctory air kisses and the hugs got over, the team from Aesthetics took over a table.

"Priya is joining us shortly. Let us keep aside the gifts for her to hand it over to the bride and the groom on behalf of the salon." Angela had barely finished her sentence when Ms Priya Kaul made her grand entry. She was the obvious head turner as many men in the crowd were caught by their wives drooling over her.

"Hello team, I hope I am not fashionably late. Has someone handed over the gifts or you all have been waiting for me to do the honours?" She picked up the gifts without waiting for anyone to respond and with all the women at her back, she headed towards Roselyn and Kanwal.

Rehan was inconspicuous in his absence. Rana, Samir and Aryan had stayed back at the table doing justice to the finger food and the soft drinks.

"Where is Rehan? Is he joining us at all?" Aryan asked them.

"He has been asked to leave the salon. You were on leave the other day when Angela served him the marching orders from Priya madam," Samir replied coolly.

"That is shocking! What happened all of a sudden?" Aryan asked Samir.

"Rehan has taken to substance abuse. Many of the clients were complaining about his erratic behaviour and a change in approach at work. Rana has taken over as the principal stylist and I will be working as his assistant," Samir answered proudly with awe in his face for his benefactor.

"I had warned Rehan that the threat was looming at large from someone waiting in the wings to take over the crown."

The arrogance in Rana was the evidence of his elevation in stature at the master outlet of Aesthetics.

The ladies had come back to the table and the men ended their conversation abruptly upon their return.

"Aryan, I need to talk to you." Bipasha stole Aryan from the group without seeking his consent.

"You must have heard that Rehan has been asked to leave and Rana has taken over as the principal stylist with immediate effect. The salon is ready to be launched in three months from now and I will be glad if you join us as the lead stylist. You can quote your price as Karan is more than keen to have you in the business as per your terms."

"Thank you Bipasha, for making the offer. I am happy that you are starting on your own because you are getting what you deserved. I am happy with the firm footing that I have managed for myself at Aesthetics. In all fairness, I would want to continue for some more time before considering a move." Aryan was firm in his decision.

"Never mind, as I always knew that you are meant for bigger things, considering your passion to excel at work." Bipasha was disappointed with Aryan's refusal of the offer but she stood on her grounds as an entrepreneur in the making.

"I have my brother Rohan who is looking for an opportunity. He has graduated with an MBA degree and has experience with sales and distribution with reputed organisations. Would you have anything for him as an offer of employment?" Aryan did not forget to seek out his priority in place.

"We would be re-selling and retailing an international brand in cosmetics and we have our plans to launch our own line of herbal products very soon. Ask him to meet up with Karan and if found suitable, he can look after the sales and distribution."

"Thank you Bipasha. I will always count you as one of my mentors." Aryan felt obliged.

"You are always welcome Aryan. If you ever have a change of mind, the doors to our place will remain open for you to be greeted as the lead stylist." Bipasha was courteous but businesslike in her taut reply.

They went back to the team at the table having missed out in noticing the roving eyes of Priya who was continuously watching them talk and she was ill at ease till they returned.

"Let us get some food," Nagma asked everyone to join her for dinner.

"Aryan, please stay back for some time. I have something to discuss with you privately," Priya spoke to Aryan for the first time since he had joined the salon.

"How are you Aryan? I am sorry, I chose not to talk to you all this while. Firstly, there was no specific need and secondly but most importantly, I know that you have a self-esteem issue. I was not sure how have you taken it to be hired at Aesthetics on my insistence," Priya clarified her stance with Aryan.

"Madam, firstly thank you for giving me the opportunity to be with Aesthetics. I needed a job very badly when this happened. I see no reason to be offended for you have rightly maintained a professional distance. I am earning my money by doing my job and neither of us can complain." Aryan was as sharp as he was known to be.

"Aryan, our paths have crossed and I am not surprised to tell you that you remain the same gentleman I admire." Priya attempted to become personal with Aryan but he was not the one to get moved as easily for he knew that she had an ulterior agenda which was yet to be spelt out.

"The salon cannot afford to lose you to an inferior proposition. Aesthetics is too big to even consider Bipasha as a competitor." Priya revealed her actual reason in asking Aryan to stay back for a conversation in private.

"I am told that you are the brain behind the astonishing success of Aesthetics. I do not understand much about the intricacies around building a business but I know one thing for sure. I am good with my work, but I am not invincible, for I do not discount the people at their face value."

"I could have considered you to be rude but I think you are no longer a hermit. You have grown worldly wise. The people at Aesthetics are the backbone of the business. I am only concerned that someone as promising as you and with your skill set should be sticking with us to make a career." Priya made her point but was careful not to create any loophole with her conversation.

Aryan decided not to play around with the words any longer. Priya had become as fragile as a glass that was waiting to crack with a little pressure. "Bipasha made an offer, which I refused."

"I am relieved as I was concerned about losing you to Bipasha. You will always be the gentleman whom I secretly admire, but I find myself wanting in something or the other to deserve you." Priya had no reservations with her admission and she left the place without saying a goodbye either to the hosts or to her team.

The team was back at the table when they noticed Priya leaving. Nagma got a plate with food for Aryan as they merrily sat down together with Roselyn and Kanwal joining them for the dinner.

"Why did she have to come when she did not even have the courtesy to say goodbye to the couple?" Nagma handed over the plate to Aryan and blurted out.

"She had come over to ensure that Aesthetics does not lose out Aryan to my venture. I am happy that she is already feeling threatened," Bipasha's remark made everyone break into laughter.

"We work to earn a living and she pays us to earn her living." It was an emboldened and the real Angela who summed it up for everyone and there were roars of cheer and laughter from everyone.

The crowd had thinned by then and the motley group of people who were left behind was the caterers and the immediate family members of the couple. Angela led the team out of the venue, leaving behind Roselyn and Kanwal with their folks. The sky was basking in the night to be lit up in a few hours to usher in a new day, so that the world got to live with its share of ecstasy and agony.

Epilogue

Rhea had come over to Kolkata for two weeks, during which the siblings bonded like never before with Ahana as an addition to their inner circle. Rhea was considering moving back to Kolkata. Rohan had started afresh and got offered the job by Karan Seth with '*Style Statements*', a newly launched unisex beauty and skin treatment salon.

Ms Priya Kaul had become one of the Directors with Aesthetics. Raghav started making headlines once again for his political maneuvers. RGV mall was getting acquired by a business consortium that was planning to revive the mall with even grander plans. The gated community remained ghostly in the absence of one of its patron who had gone missing.

Bipasha settled in her second marriage with Karan Seth and started the venture with a bang, promising many more surprises in store in the days to come. Nagma continued to be the chatterbox at the salon and offered her newly acquired knowhow on the difference between migraine and common cold. Her father was still breathing, but much better under the watchful eyes of her brother, Dr Imran Qureshi. Kanwal had started taking serious interest in the family business and was found to be less frequent with picking up Roselyn after her work due to his demanding schedule. Last heard, Rehan was steadily recovering at a drug rehabilitation center, thanks to the efforts made by Nagma.

Rana had become the numero uno stylist with Samir at his beck and call, especially to fetch him the lighter during his smoking breaks. Aryan joined him at times during the breaks as they had become fast friends. Aryan refrained from smoking at Ahana's insistence. She had also got him enrolled for computer and language classes. He was finding real merit with attending the classes besides getting pretty regular at Ahana's home, whenever they got the time to bond over the basics in their relationship. Aryan got introduced to Rajdeep, Ahana's elder brother when he came back for an extended vacation with his family.

There was still no news about Aryan's mother, Mrs Anuradha Roy Chowdhury.

The political class kept on experimenting with the newer and supposedly more effective divisive ploys in politics, the most prominent of it being the social media based divide. The media remained subtle in not declaring their political patronage. They, however, made it amply clear that it was merely a balance of equation between their profit margin and the outcome of any election.